"So we're still, technically speaking, man and wife," Xanthe clarified.

"You had better be kidding me."

"I've come all the way from London this morning to get you to sign the newly issued papers so we can fix this nightmare as fast as is humanly possible. So no, I'm not kidding." She flicked through the document until she got to the signature page, which she had already signed, frustrated when her fingers wouldn't stop trembling. She could smell him, the scent that was uniquely Dane's: clean and male and far too enticing.

She drew back. Too late. She'd already ingested a lungful, detecting expensive cedarwood soap now instead of the supermarket brand he had once used.

"Once you've signed here—" she pointed to the signature line "—*our* problem will be solved and I guarantee I'll never darken your door again." She whipped a gold pen out of the briefcase, stabbed the button at the top and thrust it toward him like a dagger.

Books by Heidi Rice

One Night, So Pregnant!
Unfinished Business with the Duke
Public Affair, Secretly Expecting
Hot-Shot Tycoon, Indecent Proposal
Pleasure, Pregnancy and a Proposition
Beach Bar Baby
Maid of Dishonor

Visit the Author Profile page at Harlequin.com for more titles.

Heidi Rice

VOWS THEY CAN'T ESCAPE

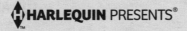

HARLEQUIN PRESENTS®

Recycling programs
for this product may
not exist in your area.

ISBN-13: 978-0-373-06044-3

Vows They Can't Escape

First North American publication 2017

Copyright © 2017 by Heidi Rice

Printed in U.S.A.

VOWS THEY CAN'T ESCAPE

With thanks to my cousin Susan, who suggested I write a romance with a female CEO as the heroine; my best writing mate Abby Green, who kept telling me to write a classic Presents; my best mate Catri, who plotted this with me on the train back from Kilkenny Shakespeare Festival; and Sarah Hornby of the Royal Thames Yacht Club, who explained why having my hero and heroine spend a night belowdecks while sailing a yacht together round the Caribbean probably wasn't a good idea!

CHAPTER ONE

XANTHE CARMICHAEL STRODE into the gleaming steel-and-glass lobby of the twenty-six-storey office block housing Redmond Design Studios on Manhattan's West Side, satisfied that the machine-gun taps of her heels against the polished stone flooring said exactly what she wanted them to say.

Watch out, boys, woman scorned on the warpath.

Ten years after Dane Redmond had abandoned her in a seedy motel room on the outskirts of Boston, she was ready to bring the final curtain crashing down on their brief and catastrophic liaison.

So the flush that had leaked into her cheeks despite the building's overefficient air conditioning and the bottomless pit opening up in her stomach could take a hike.

After a six-hour flight from Heathrow, spent power-napping in the soulless comfort of Business Class, and two days and nights figuring out how she was going to deal with the unexploded bomb the head of her legal team, Bill Spencer, had dropped at her feet on Wednesday afternoon, she was ready for any eventuality.

Whatever Dane Redmond had once meant to her

seventeen-year-old self, the potentially disastrous situation Bill had uncovered wasn't personal any more—it was business. And *nothing* got in the way of her business.

Carmichael's, the two-hundred-year-old shipping company which had been in her family for four generations, was the only thing that mattered to her now. And she would do anything to protect it and her new position as the majority shareholder and CEO.

'Hi, I'm Ms Sanders, from London, England,' she said to the immaculately dressed woman at reception, giving the false name she'd instructed her PA to use when setting up this meeting. However confident she felt, she was not about to give a barc-knuckle fighter like Dane a heads-up. 'I have an appointment with Mr Redmond to discuss a commission.'

The woman sent her a smile as immaculate as her appearance. 'It's great to meet you, Ms Sanders.' She tapped the screen in front of her and picked up the phone. 'If you'd like to take a seat, Mr Redmond's assistant, Mel Mathews, will be down in a few minutes to escort you to the eighteenth floor.'

Xanthe's heartbeat thudded against her collarbone as she recrossed the lobby under the life-size model of a huge wing sail catamaran suspended from the ceiling. A polished brass plaque announced that the boat had won Redmond Design a prestigious sailing trophy twice in a row.

She resisted the urge to chew off the lipstick she'd applied in the cab ride from JFK.

Bill's bombshell would have been less problematic

if Dane had still been the boy her father had so easily dismissed as 'a trailer trash wharf rat with no class and fewer prospects,' but she refused to be cowed by Dane's phenomenal success over the last decade.

She was here to show him who he was dealing with.

But, as she took in the ostentatious design of Dane's new headquarters in New York's uber-hip Meatpacking District, the awe-inspiring view of the Hudson River from the lobby's third-floor aspect and that beast of a boat, she had to concede the meteoric rise of his business and his position as one of the world's premier sailing boat designers didn't surprise her.

He'd always been smart and ambitious—a natural-born sailor more at home on water than dry land—which was exactly why her father's estate manager had hired him that summer in Martha's Vineyard to run routine maintenance on the small fleet of two yachts and a pocket cruiser her father kept at their holiday home.

Running routine maintenance on Charles Carmichael's impressionable, naive daughter had been done on his own time.

No one had ever been able to fault Dane's work ethic.

Xanthe's thigh muscles trembled at the disturbingly vivid memory of blunt fingers trailing across sensitive skin, but she didn't break stride.

All that energy and purpose had drawn her to him like a heat-seeking missile. That and the superpower they'd discovered together—his unique ability to lick her to a scream-your-lungs-out orgasm in sixty seconds or less.

She propped her briefcase on a coffee table and sank into one of the leather chairs lining the lobby.

Whoa, Xan. Do not think about the superpower.

Crossing her legs, she squeezed her knees together, determined to halt the conflagration currently converging on the hotspot between her thighs. Even Dane's superpower would never be enough to compensate for the pain he'd caused.

She hid the unsettling thought behind a tight smile as a thirtysomething woman headed in her direction across the ocean of polished stone. Grabbing the briefcase containing the documents she had flown three thousand miles to deliver, Xanthe stood up, glad when her thighs remained virtually quiver-free.

Dane Redmond's not the only badass in town. Not any more.

Xanthe was feeling less like a badass and more like a sacrificial lamb five minutes later, as the PA led her through a sea of hip and industrious young marketing people working on art boards and computers on the eighteenth floor. Even her machine-gun heel taps had been muffled by the industrial carpeting.

The adrenaline which had been pumping through her veins for forty-eight hours and keeping her upright slowed to a crawl as they approached the glass-walled corner office and the man within, silhouetted against the New Jersey shoreline. The jolt of recognition turned the bottomless pit in her stomach into a yawning chasm.

Broad shoulders and slim hips were elegantly attired in steel-grey trousers and a white shirt. But his imposing height, the muscle bulk revealed by the shirt's rolled-up sleeves, the dark buzz cut hugging the dome of his skull, and the tattoo that covered his left arm down to his elbow did nothing to disguise the wolf in expensively tailored clothing.

Sweat gathered between Xanthe's breasts and the powder-blue silk suit and peach camisole ensemble she'd chosen twelve hours ago in London, because it covered all the bases from confident to kick-ass, rubbed against her skin like sandpaper.

The internet hadn't done Dane Redmond justice. Because the memory of the few snatched images she'd found yesterday while preparing for this meeting was comprehensively failing to stop a boulder the size of an asteroid forming in her throat.

She forced one foot in front of the other as the PA tapped on the office door and led her into the wolf's den.

Brutally blue eyes locked on Xanthe's face.

A flicker of stunned disbelief softened his rugged features before his jaw went rigid, making the shallow dent in his chin twitch. The searing look had the thundering beat of Xanthe's heart dropping into that yawning chasm.

Had she actually kidded herself that age and money and success would have refined Dane—tamed him, even—or at the very least made him a lot less intense and intimidating? Because she'd been dead wrong. Either that or she'd just been struck by lightning.

'This is Ms Sanders from—'

'Leave us, Mel.' Dane interrupted the PA's introduction. 'And shut the door.'

The husky command had Xanthe's heartbeat galloping into her throat to party with the asteroid, reminding her of all the commands he'd once issued to her in the same he-who-shall-be-obeyed tone. And the humiliating speed with which she'd obeyed them.

'Relax, I won't hurt you. I swear.'

'Hold on tight. This is gonna be the ride of your life.'

'I take care of my own, Xan. That's non-negotiable.'

The door closed behind the dutiful PA with a hushed click.

Xanthe gripped the handle on her briefcase with enough force to crack a nail and lifted her chin, channelling the smouldering remains of her inner badass that had survived the lightning strike.

'Hello, Dane,' she said, glad when her voice remained relatively steady.

She would *not* be derailed by a physical reaction which was ten years out of date and nothing more than an inconvenient throwback to her youth. It would pass. Eventually.

'Hello, *Ms Sanders*.'

His thinly veiled contempt at her deception had outrage joining the riot of other emotions she was busy trying to suppress.

'If you've come to buy a boat, you're all out of luck.'

The searing gaze wandered down to her toes, the insolent appraisal as infuriating as the fuses that flared to life in every pulse point en route.

'I don't do business with spoilt little rich chicks.'

His gaze rose back to her face, having laid waste to her composure.

'Especially ones I was once dumb enough to marry.'

CHAPTER TWO

Xanthe Carmichael.

Dane Redmond had just taken a sucker punch to the gut. And it was taking every ounce of his legendary control not to show it.

The girl who had haunted his dreams a lifetime ago—particularly all his wet dreams—and then become a star player in his nightmares. And now she had the balls to stand in his office—the place he'd built from the ground up after she'd kicked him to the kerb—as if she had a right to invade his life a second time.

She'd changed some from the girl he remembered—all trussed-up now in a snooty suit, looking chic and classy in those ice-pick heels. But there was enough of that girl left to force him to put his libido on lockdown.

She still had those wide, feline eyes. Their sultry slant hinting at the banked fires beneath, the translucent blue-green the vivid colour of the sea over the Barrier Reef. She had the same peaches-and-cream complexion, with the sprinkle of girlish freckles over her nose she hadn't quite managed to hide under a smooth mask of make-up. And that riot of red-gold hair, ruthlessly styled now in an updo, but for a few strands that had escaped to cling to her neck and draw his gaze to the coy hint of cleavage beneath her suit.

The flush high on her cheekbones and the glitter in her eyes made her look like a fairy queen who had swallowed a cockroach. But he knew she was worse than any siren sent to lure men to their destruction, with that stunning body and that butter-wouldn't-melt expression—and about as much freaking integrity as a sea serpent.

He curled his twitching fingers into his palms and braced his fists against the desk. Because part of him wanted to throw her over his knee and spank her until her butt was as red as her hair, and another part of him longed to throw her over his shoulder and take her somewhere dark and private, so he could rip off that damn suit and find the responsive girl beneath who had once begged him for release.

And each one of those impulses was as screwed-up as the other. Because she meant nothing to him now. Not a damn thing. And he'd sworn ten years ago, when he'd been lying on the road outside her father's vacation home in the Vineyard, with three busted ribs, more bruises than even his old man had given him on a bad day, his stomach hollow with grief and tight with anger and humiliation, that no woman would ever make such a jackass of him again.

'I'm here because we have a problem…' She hesitated, her lip trembling ever so slightly.

She was nervous. She ought to be.

'Which I'm here to solve.'

'How could *we* possibly have a problem?' he said, his voice deceptively mild. 'When *we* haven't seen each other in over a decade and I never wanted to see you again?'

She stiffened, the flush spreading down her neck to highlight the lush valley of her breasts.

'The feeling's mutual,' she said. The snotty tone was a surprise.

He buried his fists into his pants pockets. The last thin thread controlling his temper about to snap.

Where the heck did she get off, being pissed with him? *He'd* been the injured party in their two-second marriage. She'd flaunted herself, come on to him, had him panting after her like a dog that whole summer— hooked him like a prize tuna by promising to love, honour and obey him, no matter what. Then she'd run back to daddy at the first sign of trouble. Not that he'd been dumb enough to really believe those breathless promises. He'd learned when he was still a kid that love was just an empty sentiment. But he *had* been dumb enough to trust her.

And now she had the gall to turn up at *his* place, under a false name, expecting him to be polite and pretend what she'd done was okay.

Whatever her problem was, he wanted no part of it. But he'd let her play out this little drama before he slapped her down and kicked her the hell out of his life. For good this time.

Lifting her briefcase onto the table, Xanthe ignored the hostility radiating from the man in front of her. She flipped the locks, whipped out the divorce papers and slapped them on the desk.

Dane Redmond's caveman act was nothing new, but she was wise to it now. He'd been exactly the same as a nineteen-year-old. Taciturn and bossy and supremely arrogant. Once upon a time she'd found that wildly attractive—because once upon a time she'd believed that lurking beneath the caveman was a boy who'd needed the love she could lavish on him.

That had been her first mistake. Followed by too many others.

The vulnerable boy had never existed. And the caveman had never wanted what she had to offer.

Good thing, then, that this wasn't about him any more—it was about *her*. And what *she* wanted. Which was exactly what she was going to get.

Because no man bullied her now. Not her father, not the board of directors at Carmichael's and certainly not some overly ripped boat designer who thought he could boss her around just because she'd once been bewitched by his larger-than-average penis.

'The problem is...' She threw the papers onto the desk, cursing the tremor in her fingers at that sudden recollection of Dane fully aroused.

Do not think about him naked.

'My father's solicitor, Augustus Greaves, failed to file the paperwork for our divorce ten years ago.'

She delivered the news in a rush, to disguise any hint of culpability. It was not her fault Greaves had been an alcoholic.

'So we're still, technically speaking, man and wife.'

CHAPTER THREE

'You had better be freaking kidding me!'

Dane looked so shocked Xanthe would have smiled if she hadn't been shaking quite so hard. That had certainly wiped the self-righteous glare off his face.

'I've come all the way from London to get you to sign these newly issued papers, so we can fix this nightmare as fast as is humanly possible. So, no, I'm not kidding.'

She flicked through the document until she got to the signature page, which she had already signed, frustrated because her fingers wouldn't stop trembling. She could smell him—that scent that was uniquely his, clean and male, and far too enticing.

She drew back. Too late. She'd already ingested a lungful, detecting expensive cedarwood soap instead of the supermarket brand he had once used.

'Once you've signed here—' she pointed to the signature line '—*our* problem will be solved and I can guarantee never to darken your door again.'

She whipped a gold pen out of the briefcase, stabbed the button at the top and thrust it towards him like a dagger.

He lifted his hands out of his pockets but didn't pick up the gauntlet.

'Like I'd be dumb enough to sign anything *you* put in front of me without checking it first...'

She ruthlessly controlled the snap of temper at his statement. And the wave of panic.

Stay calm. Be persuasive. Don't freak out.

She breathed in through her nose and out through her mouth, employing the technique she'd perfected during the last five years of handling Carmichael's board. As long as Dane never found out about the original terms of her father's will, nothing in the paperwork she'd handed him would clue him in to the *real* reason she'd come all this way. And why would he, when her father's will hadn't come into force until five years after Dane had abandoned her?

Unfortunately the memory of that day in her father's office, with her stomach cramping in shock and loss and disbelief as the executor recited the terms of the will, was not helping with her anxiety attack.

'Your father had hoped you would marry one of the candidates he suggested. His first preference was to leave forty-five per cent of Carmichael's stock to you and the controlling share to your spouse as the new CEO. As no such marriage was contracted at the time of his death, he has put the controlling share in trust, to be administered by the board until you complete a five-year probationary period as Carmichael's executive owner. If, after that period, they deem you a credible CEO, they can vote to allocate a further six per cent of

*the shares to you. If not, they can elect another CEO
and leave the shares in trust.'*

That deadline had passed a week ago. The board—no
doubt against all her father's expectations—had voted
in her favour. And then Bill had discovered his bombshell—that she had still technically been married to
Dane at the time of her father's death and he could,
therefore, sue for the controlling share in the company.

It might almost have been funny—that her father's lack
of trust in her abilities might end up gifting 55 per cent
of his company to a man he had despised—if it hadn't
been more evidence that her father had never trusted her
with Carmichael's.

She pushed the dispiriting thought to one side, and
the echo of grief that came with it, as Dane punched a
number into his smartphone.

Her father might have been old-fashioned and hopelessly traditional—an aristocratic Englishman who believed that no man who hadn't gone to Eton and Oxford
could ever be a suitable husband for her—but he had
loved her and had wanted the best for her. Once she
got Dane to sign on the dotted line, thus eliminating
any possible threat this paperwork error could present
to her father's company—*her* company—she would
finally have proved her commitment to Carmichael's
was absolute.

'Jack? I've got something I want you to check out.'
Dane beckoned to someone behind Xanthe as he spoke
into the phone. The superefficient PA popped back into
the office as if by magic. 'Mel is gonna send it over by
messenger.'

He handed the document to his PA, then scribbled something on a pad and passed that to her, too. The PA trotted out.

'Make sure you check every line,' he continued, still talking to whomever was on the other end of the phone. He gave a strained chuckle. 'Not exactly—it's *supposed* to be divorce papers.'

The judgmental once-over he gave Xanthe had her temper rising up her torso.

'I'll explain the why and the how another time,' he said. 'Just make sure there are no surprises—like a hidden claim for ten years' back-alimony.'

He clicked off the phone and shoved it into his pocket.

She was actually speechless. For about two seconds.

'Are you finished?' Indignation burned, the breathing technique history.

She'd come all this way, spent several sleepless nights preparing for this meeting while being constantly tormented by painful memories from that summer, not to mention having to deal with his scent and the inappropriate heat that would not die. And through it all she'd remained determined to keep this process dignified, despite the appalling way he had treated her. And he'd shot it all to hell in less than five minutes.

The arrogant ass.

'Don't play the innocent with me,' he continued, the self-righteous glare returning. 'Because I know just what you're capable—'

'You son of a...' She gasped for breath, outrage consuming her. 'I'm not *allowed* to play the innocent?

When you took my virginity, carried on seducing me all summer, got me pregnant, insisted I marry you and then dumped me three months later?'

He'd never told her he loved her—never even tried to see her point of view during their one and only argument. But, worse than that, he hadn't been there when she had needed him the most. Her stomach churned, the in-flight meal she'd picked at on the plane threatening to gag her as misery warred with fury, bringing the memories flooding back—memories which were too painful to forget even though she'd tried.

The pungent smell of mould and cheap disinfectant in the motel bathroom, the hazy sight of the cracked linoleum through the blur of tears, the pain hacking her in two as she prayed for him to pick up his phone.

Dane's face went completely blank, before a red stain of fury lanced across the tanned cheekbones. '*I* dumped *you*? Are you *nuts*?' he yelled at top volume.

'You walked out and left me in that motel room and you didn't answer my calls.' She matched him decibel for decibel. She wasn't that besotted girl any more, too timid and delusional to stand up and fight her corner. 'What *else* would you call it?'

'I was two hundred miles out at sea, crewing on a bluefin tuna boat—that's what I'd call it. I didn't get your calls because there isn't a heck of a lot of network coverage in the middle of the North Atlantic. And when I got back a week later I found out you'd hightailed it back to daddy because of one damn disagreement.'

The revelation of where he'd been while she'd been losing their baby gave her pause—but only for a moment. He could have rung her to tell her about the job *before* he'd boarded the boat, but in his typical don't-ask-don't-tell fashion he hadn't. And what about the frantic message she'd left him while she'd waited for her father to arrive and take her to the emergency room? And later, when she'd come round from the fever dreams back in her bedroom on her father's estate?

She'd asked the staff to contact Dane, to tell him about the baby, her heart breaking into a thousand pieces, but he'd never even responded to the news. Except to send through the signed divorce papers weeks later.

She could have forgiven him for not caring about *her*. Their marriage had been the definition of a shotgun wedding, the midnight elopement a crazy adventure hyped up on teenage hormones, testosterone-fuelled bravado and the mad panic caused by an unplanned pregnancy. But it was his failure to care about the three-month-old life which had died inside her, his failure to even be willing to mourn its passing, that she couldn't forgive.

It had tortured her for months. How many lies he'd told about being there for her, respecting her decision to have the baby. How he'd even gone through with their farce of a marriage, while all the time planning to dump her at the first opportunity.

It had made no sense to her for so long—until she'd finally figured it out. Why he'd always deflected conversations about the future, about the baby. Why he'd never once returned her declarations of love even while stoking the sexual heat between them to fever pitch. Why he'd stormed out that morning after her innocent

suggestion that she look for a job, too, because she knew
he was struggling to pay their motel bill.

He'd gotten bored with the marriage, with the responsibility. And sex had been the only thing binding
them together. He'd never wanted her or the baby. His
offer of marriage had been a knee-jerk reaction he'd
soon regretted. And once she'd lost the baby he'd had
the perfect excuse he'd been looking for to discard her.

That truth had devastated her at the time. Brought
her to her knees. How could she have been so wrong
about him? About *them*? But it had been a turning point,
too. Because she'd survived the loss, repaired her shattered heart, and made herself into the woman she was
now—someone who didn't rely on others to make herself whole.

Thanks to Dane's carelessness, his neglect, she'd shut
off her stupid, fragile, easily duped heart and found a
new purpose—devoting herself to the company that was
her legacy. She'd begged her father for a lowly internship
position that autumn, when they'd returned to London,
and begun working her backside off to learn everything she needed to know about Europe's top maritime
logistics brand.

At first it had been a distraction, a means of avoiding the great big empty space inside her. But eventually
she'd stopped simply going through the motions and actually found something to care about again. She'd aced
her MBA, learnt French and Spanish while working in
Carmichael's subsidiary offices in Calais and Cadiz,
and even managed to persuade her father to give her a
job at the company's head office in Whitehall before

he'd died—all the while fending off his attempts to find her a 'suitable' husband.

She'd earned the position she had now through hard work and dedication and toughened up enough to take charge of her life. So there was no way on earth she was going to back down from this fight and let Dane Redmond lay some ludicrous guilt trip on her when *he* was the one who had crushed her and every one of her hopes and dreams. Maybe they had been foolish hopes and stupid pipe dreams, but the callous way he'd done it had been unnecessarily cruel.

'You promised to be there for me,' she shot back, her fury going some way to mask the hollow pain in her stomach. The same pain she'd sworn never to feel again. 'You swore you would protect me and support me. But when I needed you the most you weren't there.'

'What the hell did you need *me* there for?' he spat the words out, the brittle light in the icy blue eyes shocking her into silence.

The fight slammed out of her lungs on a gasp of breath.

Because in that moment all she could see was his rage.

The hollow pain became sharp and jagged, tearing through the last of her resistance until all that was left was the horrifying uncertainty that had crippled her as a teenager.

Why was he so angry with her? When all she'd ever done was try to love him?

'I wanted you to be there for me when I lost our

baby,' she whispered, her voice sounding as if it were coming from another dimension.

'You wanted me to hold your hand while you aborted my kid?'

'What?' His sarcasm, the sneered disbelief sliced through her, and the jagged pain exploded into something huge.

'You think I don't *know* you got rid of it?'

The accusation in his voice, the contempt, suddenly made a terrible kind of sense.

'But I—' She tried to squeeze the words past the asteroid in her throat.

He cut her off. 'I hitched a ride straight to the Vineyard once I got back on shore. We'd had that fight and you'd left some garbled message on my cell. When I got to your old man's place he told me there was no baby any more, showed me the divorce papers you'd signed and then had me kicked out. And that's when I figured out the truth. Daddy's little princess had decided that my kid was an inconvenience she didn't need.'

She didn't see hatred any more, just a seething resentment, but she couldn't process any of it. His words buzzed round in her brain like mutant bees which refused to land. *Had* she signed the divorce papers first? She couldn't remember doing that. All she could remember was begging to see Dane, and her father showing her Dane's signature on the documents. And how the sight of his name scrawled in black ink had killed the last tiny remnant of hope still lurking inside her.

'I know the pregnancy was a mistake. Hell, the whole damn marriage was insane,' Dane continued, his tone caustic with disgust. 'And if you'd told me that's what you'd decided to do I would have tried to understand. But you didn't have the guts to own it, did you? You didn't even have the guts to tell me that's what you'd done? So don't turn up here and pretend you were some innocent kid, seduced by the big bad wolf. Because we both know that's garbage. There was only *one* innocent party in the whole screwed-up mess of our marriage and it wasn't either one of us.'

She could barely hear him, those mutant killer bees had become a swarm. Her legs began to shake, and the jagged pain in her stomach joined the thudding cacophony in her skull. She locked her knees, wrapped her arms around her midriff and swallowed convulsively, trying to prevent the silent screams from vomiting out of her mouth.

How could you not know how much our baby meant to me?

'What's wrong?' Dane demanded, the contempt turning to reluctant concern.

She tried to force her shattered thoughts into some semblance of order. But the machete embedded in her head was about to split her skull in two. And she couldn't form the words.

'Damn it, Red, you look as if you're about to pass out.'

Firm hands clamped on her upper arms and became the only thing keeping her upright as her knees buckled.

The old nickname and the shock of his touch had a blast of memory assaulting her senses—hurtling her back in time to those stolen days on the water in Buzzards Bay: the hot sea air, the shrieks of the cormorants, the scent of salt mixed with the funky aroma of sweat and sex, the devastating joy as his calloused fingers brought her body to vibrant life.

I didn't have an abortion.

She tried to force the denial free from the stranglehold in her throat, but nothing came out.

I had a miscarriage.

She heard him curse, felt firm fingers digging into her biceps as the cacophony in her head became deafening. And she stepped over the edge to let herself fall.

CHAPTER FOUR

WHAT THE—?

Dane leapt forward as Xanthe's eyes rolled back, scooping her dead weight into his arms before she could crash to earth.

'Is Ms Sanders sick?' Mel appeared, her face blank with shock.

'Her name's Carmichael.'

Or, technically speaking, Redmond.

He barged past his PA, cradling Xanthe against his chest. 'Call Dr Epstein and tell him to meet me in the penthouse.'

'What—what shall I say happened?' Mel stammered, nowhere near as steady as usual.

He knew how she felt. His palms were sweating, his pulse racing fast enough to win the Kentucky Derby.

Xanthe let out a low moan. He tightened his grip, something hot and fluid hitting him as his fingertips brushed her breast.

'I don't know what happened,' he replied. 'Just tell Epstein to get up there.'

He threw the words over his shoulder as he strode

through the office, past his sponsorship and marketing team, every one of whom was staring at him as if he'd just told them the company had declared bankruptcy.

Had they heard him shouting at Red like a madman? Letting the fury he'd buried years ago spew out of his mouth?

Where had that come from?

He'd lost it—and he *never* lost it. Not since the day on her father's estate when he'd gone berserk, determined to see Xanthe no matter what her father said.

Of course he hadn't told her that part of the story. The part where he'd made an ass of himself.

The pulse already pounding in his temple began to throb like a wound. He'd been dog-tired and frantic with worry when he'd arrived at Carmichael's vacation home, his pride in tatters, his gut clenching at the thought Xanthe had run out on him.

All that had made him easy prey for the man who hadn't considered him fit to kiss the hem of his precious daughter's bathrobe, let alone marry her. He could still see Charles Carmichael's smug expression, hear that superior I'm-better-than-you tone as the guy told him their baby was gone and that his daughter had made the sensible decision to cut all ties with the piece of trailer trash she should never have married.

The injustice of it all, the sense of loss, the futile anger had opened up a great big black hole inside him that had been waiting to drag him under ever since he was a little boy. So he'd exploded with rage—and got his butt thoroughly kicked by Carmichael's goons for his trouble.

Obviously some of that rage was still lurking in his subconscious. Or he wouldn't have freaked out again. Over something that meant nothing now.

He'd been captivated by Xanthe that summer. By her cute accent, the sexy, subtle curves rocking the bikini-shorts-and-T-shirt combos she'd lived in, her quick, curious mind and most of all the artless flirting that had grown hotter and hotter until they'd made short work of those bikini shorts.

The obvious crush she'd had on him had flattered him, had made him feel like somebody when everyone else treated him like a nobody. But their connection had never been about anything other than hot sex—souped up to fever pitch by teenage lust. He knew he'd been nuts to think it could ever be more, especially once she'd run back to Daddy when she'd discovered what it was *really* like to live on a waterman's pay.

Xanthe stirred, her fragrant hair brushing his chin.

'Settle down. I've got you.' A wave of protectiveness washed over him. He didn't plan to examine it too closely. She'd been his responsibility once. She wasn't his responsibility any more. Whatever the paperwork said.

This was old news. It didn't make a damn bit of difference now. Obviously the shock of seeing her again had worked stuff loose which had been hanging about without his knowledge.

'Where are you taking me?'

The groggy question brought him back to the problem nestled in his arms.

He elbowed the call button on the elevator, grateful

when the doors zipped open and they could get out of range of their audience. Stepping inside, he nudged the button marked Penthouse Only.

'My place. Top floor.'

'What happened?'

He glanced down to find her eyes glazed, her face still pale as a ghost. She looked sweet and innocent and scared—the way she had once before.

'It's positive. I'm going to have a baby. What are we going to do?'

He concentrated on the panel above his head, shoving the flashback where it belonged—in the file marked Ancient History.

'You tell me.' He kept his voice casual. 'One minute we were yelling at each other and the next you were hitting the deck.'

'I must have fainted,' she said, as if she wasn't sure. She shifted, colour flooding back into her cheeks. 'You can put me down now. I'm fine.'

He should do what she asked, because having her soft curves snug against his chest and that sultry scent filling his nostrils wasn't doing much for his equilibrium, but his heartbeat was still going for gold in Kentucky.

His grip tightened.

'Uh-huh?' He raised a sceptical eyebrow. 'You make a habit of swooning like a heroine in a trashy novel?'

Her chin took on a mutinous tilt, but she didn't reply.

Finally, score one to Redmond.

The elevator arrived at his penthouse and the doors opened onto the panoramic view of the downtown skyline.

At any other time the sight would have brought with it a satisfying ego-boost. The designer furniture, the modern steel and glass structure and the expertly planted roof terrace, its lap pool sparkling in the fading sunlight, was a million miles away from the squalid dump he'd grown up in. He'd worked himself raw in the last couple of years, and spent a huge chunk of investment capital, to complete the journey.

But he wasn't feeling too proud of himself at the moment. He'd lost his temper downstairs, but worse than that, he'd let his emotions get the upper hand.

'Stop crying like a girl and get me another beer, or you'll be even sorrier than you are already, you little pissant.'

His old man had been a mean drunk, whom he'd grown to despise, but one thing the hard bastard had taught him was that letting your emotions show only made you weak.

Xanthe had completed his education by teaching him another valuable lesson—that mixing sex with sentiment was never a good idea.

Somehow both those lessons had deserted him downstairs.

He deposited her on the leather couch in the centre of the living space and stepped back, aware of the persistent ache in his crotch.

She got busy fussing with her hair, not meeting his eyes. Her staggered breathing made her breasts swell against the lacy top. The persistent ache spiked.

Terrific.

'Thank you,' she said. 'But you didn't have to carry me all the way up here.'

She looked around the space, still not meeting his eyes.

He stifled the disappointment when she didn't comment on the apartment. He wasn't looking for her approval. Certainly didn't need it.

'The company doc's coming up to check you out,' he said.

That got her attention. Her gaze flashed to his— equal parts aggravation and embarrassment.

'That's not necessary. It's just a bit of jet lag.'

Jet lag didn't make all the colour drain out of your face, or give your eyes that haunted, hunted look. And it sure as hell didn't make you drop like a stone in the middle of an argument.

'Tell that to Dr Epstein.'

She was getting checked out by a professional whether she liked it or not. She might not be his responsibility any more, but this was his place and his rules.

The elevator bell dinged on cue.

He crossed the apartment to greet the doctor, his racing heartbeat finally reaching the finish line and heading into a victory lap when he heard Xanthe's annoyed huff of breath behind him.

Better to deal with a pissed Xanthe than one who fainted dead away right before his eyes.

CHAPTER FIVE

'WHAT I'M PRESCRIBING is a balanced meal and a solid ten hours' sleep, in that order.'

The good Dr Epstein sent Xanthe a grave look which made her feel as if she were four years old again, being chastised by Nanny Foster for refusing to go down for her nap.

'Your blood pressure is elevated and the fact you haven't eaten or slept well in several days is no doubt the cause of this episode. Stress is a great leveller, Ms Carmichael,' he added.

As if she didn't know that, with the source of her stress standing two feet away, eavesdropping.

This was *so* not what she needed right now. For Dane to know that she hadn't had a good night's sleep or managed to eat a full meal since Wednesday morning. Thanks to the good doctor's interrogation she might as well be wearing a sign with Weak and Feeble Woman emblazoned across it.

She'd never fainted before in her life. Well, not since—

She cut off the thought.

Do not go back there. Not again.

Rehashing those dark days had already cost her far too much ground. Swooning 'like a heroine in a trashy novel,' as Dane had so eloquently put it, had done the rest. The only good thing to come out of her dying swan act was the fact that it had happened before she'd had the chance to blurt out the truth about her miscarriage.

After coming round in Dane's arms, her cheek nestled against his rock-solid shoulder and her heart thundering in her chest, the inevitable blast of heat had been followed by a much needed blast of rational thought.

She was here to finish things with Dane—not kick-start loads of angst from the past. Absolutely nothing would be achieved by correcting Dane's assumption now, other than to cast her yet again in the role of the sad, insecure little girl who needed a man to protect her.

Maybe that had been true then. Her father's high-handed decision to prevent her from seeing Dane had robbed them both of the chance to end their relationship amicably. And then her father had mucked things up completely by hiring his useless old school chum Augustus Greaves to handle the admin on the divorce.

But her father was dead now. And with hindsight she could see that in his own misguided, paternalistic way he had probably believed he was acting in her best interests. And the truth was the end result, however agonising it had been to go through at the time, *had* been in her best interests.

Who was to say she wouldn't have gone back to Dane? Been delusional enough to carry on trying to make a go of a marriage that had been a mistake from the start?

Nothing would be gained by telling Dane the truth now, ten years too late. Except to give him another golden opportunity to demonstrate his me-Tarzan-you-Jane routine.

She'd found his dominance and overprotectiveness romantic that summer. Believing it proved how much he loved her. When all it had really proved was that Dane, like her father, had never seen her as an equal.

The fact that she'd felt safe and cherished and turned on by the ease with which he'd held her a moment ago was just her girly hormones talking. And those little snitches didn't need any more excuses to join the party.

Much better that Dane respected her based on a misconception, even if it made him hate her, than that she encourage his pity with the truth. Because his pity had left her confidence and her self-esteem in the toilet ten years ago—and led to a series of stupid decisions that had nearly destroyed her.

She was a pragmatist now—a shrewd, focused career woman. One melodramatic swoon brought on by starvation and exhaustion and stress didn't change that. Thank goodness she wasn't enough of a ninny to be looking for love to complete her life any more. Because it was complete enough already.

Maybe there was a tiny tug of regret at the thought of that young man who had come to her father's estate looking for her, only to be turned away. But the fact that he'd come to the worst possible conclusion proved he'd never truly understood her. How could he *ever* have believed she would abort their child?

'I appreciate your advice, Doctor,' she replied, as the man packed the last of his paraphernalia into his bag. 'I'll make sure I grab something to eat at the airport and get some sleep on the plane.'

No doubt she'd sleep like the dead, given the emotional upheaval she'd just endured.

She glanced at her watch and stood up, steadying herself against the sofa when a feeling of weightlessness made her head spin.

'You're flying back tonight?' The doctor frowned at her again, as if she'd just thrown a tantrum.

'Yes, at seven,' she replied. She only had an hour before boarding closed on her flight to Heathrow. 'So I should get going.'

The elderly man's grave expression became decidedly condescending. 'I wouldn't advise catching a transatlantic flight tonight. You need to give yourself some time to recover. You've just had a full-blown anxiety attack.'

'A...*what*?' she yelped, far too aware of Dane's overbearing presence in her peripheral vision as he listened to every word. 'It wasn't an anxiety attack. It was just a bit of light-headedness.'

'Mr Redmond said you became very emotional, then collapsed, and that you were out for over a minute. That's more than light-headedness.'

'Right...well, thanks for your opinion, Doctor.' As if she cared what 'Mr Redmond' had to say on the subject.

'You're welcome, Ms Carmichael.'

She hung back as Dane showed Dr Epstein out, silently fuming at the subtle put-down. And the fact Dane had witnessed it. And the even bigger problem that she was going to have to wait now until the doctor had taken the lift down before she could leave herself. Which would mean spending torturous minutes alone with Dane while trying to avoid the parade of circus elephants crammed into his palatial penthouse apartment with them.

She didn't want to talk about their past, her so-called anxiety attack, or any of the other ten-ton pachyderms that might be up for discussion.

However nonchalant she'd tried to be with Dr Epstein, she *didn't* feel 100 per cent. She was shattered. The last few days *had* been stressful—more stressful than she'd wanted to admit. And the revelations that had come during their argument downstairs hadn't exactly reduced her stress levels.

And, while she was playing Truth or Dare with herself, she might as well also admit that being in Dane's office had been unsettling enough.

Being alone with him in his apartment was worse.

She shrugged into the jacket she'd taken off while Dr Epstein took her blood pressure. Time to make a dignified and speedy exit.

'Where's my briefcase?' she asked, her voice more high-pitched than she would have liked, as Dane walked back towards her.

'My office.'

He leaned against the steel banister of a staircase leading to a mezzanine level and crossed his arms over that wide chest. His stance looked relaxed. She wasn't fooled.

'I couldn't scoop it up,' he continued, his silent censure doing nothing for the pulse punching her throat, 'because I had my hands full scooping up *you*.'

'I'll get it on my way out,' she said, deliberately ignoring the sarcasm while marching towards the elevator.

He unfolded his arms and stepped into her path. 'That's not what the doctor ordered.'

'He's not *my* doctor,' she announced, distracted by the pectoral muscles outlined by creased white cotton. 'And I don't take orders.'

His sensual lips flattened into a stubborn line and his jaw hardened, drawing her attention back to the dent in his chin.

She bit into her tongue, assaulted by the sudden urge to lick that masculine dip.

What the heck?

She tried to sidestep him. He stepped with her, forcing her to butt into the wall o' pecs. Awareness shot up her spine as she took a hasty step back.

'Get out of my way.'

'Red, chill out.'

She caught a glimpse of concern, her pulse spiking uncomfortably at his casual use of the old nickname.

'I will not chill out. I have a flight to catch.' She sounded shrill, but she was starting to feel light-headed again. If she did another smackdown in front of him the last of her dignity would be in shreds.

'You're shaking.'

'I'm *not* shaking.'

Of course she was shaking. He was standing too close, crowding her, engulfing her in that subtly sexy scent. Even though he wasn't touching her she could feel him everywhere—in her tender breasts, her ragged breathing and in the hotspot between her thighs which was about to spontaneously combust. Basically, her body had reverted to its default position whenever Dane Redmond was within a ten-mile radius.

'Unless you've got a chopper handy, you've already missed your flight,' he observed, doing that sounding reasonable thing again, which made her sound hysterical. 'Midtown traffic is a bitch at this time of day. No way are you going to make it to JFK in under an hour.'

'Then I'll wait at the airport for another flight.'

'Why not hang out here and catch a flight out tomorrow like Epstein suggested?'

With him? In his apartment? Alone? Was he bonkers?

'No, thank you.'

She tried to shift round him again. A restraining hand cupped her elbow and electricity zapped up her arm.

She yanked free, the banked heat in his cool blue gaze almost as disturbing as what he said next.

'How about I apologise?'

'What for?'

Was he serious? Dane had been the original never-give-in-never-surrender guy back in the day. She'd never seen him back down or apologise for anything.

'For yelling at you in my office. About stuff that doesn't matter any more.'

It was the last thing she had expected. But as she searched his expression she could see he meant it.

It was an olive branch. She wanted to snatch it and run straight for the moral high ground. But the tug of regret in the pit of her stomach chose that precise moment to give a sharp yank.

'You don't have to apologise for speaking your mind. But, if you insist, I should apologise, too,' she continued. 'You're right. I should have consulted you about... about the abortion.'

The lie tasted sour—a betrayal of the tiny life she'd once yearned to hold in her arms. But this was the only way to finally release them both from all those foolish dreams.

'Hell, Red. You don't have to apologise for that.'

He scrubbed his hands over his scalp, the frustrated gesture bringing an old memory to the surface of running her hands over the soft bristles while they lay together on the deck of the pocket cruiser, her body pleasantly numb with afterglow from the first time they'd made love.

She pressed tingling palms against the fabric of her skirt, trying to erase the picture in her head, but the unguarded memory continued to play out—one agonising sensation at a time. Goosebumps pebbling her arms from the warm breeze off the ocean...the base of her thumb stinging from the affectionate nip as he bit into the tender flesh.

'You sure you're okay? I didn't hurt you? You're so small and delicate...'

'I get why you did it,' Dane continued, as the erotic

memory played havoc with her senses. 'You weren't ready to be a mom, and I would have been a disaster as a dad.'

He was telling her he agreed with her. Case comprehensively closed. But what should have been a victory only made the sour taste in her mouth turn to mud.

She *had* been ready to be a mother. How could he have doubted that? Didn't he *know* how much she had wanted their baby? And why would he think he'd make a terrible father? Was this something to do with all his scars, the childhood and the family he had never been willing to talk about?

Good grief, get real. You are not *still invested in that fairytale.*

The idiotic notion that she could rescue him by helping him to overcome stuff he refused to talk about had been the domain of that romantic teenage girl. That fairytale was part of her past. A past she'd just lied through her teeth to put behind her. This had to be the jet lag talking again, because it was not like her to lose her grip on reality twice in one day.

'I'd really like to settle this amicably,' she said at last, determined to accept his olive branch.

'We can do that—but you need to stay put tonight. You took a couple of years off my life downstairs, and you still look as if a strong breeze could blow you over.'

That searing gaze drifted to the top of her hair, which probably looked as if a chinchilla had been nesting in it. Awareness shimmered, the sharp tug in her abdomen ever more insistent.

'I feel responsible for that,' he said, the gentle tone at odds with the bunched muscle jumping in his jaw.

'I told you. I'm okay.' She couldn't stay. Couldn't risk becoming that poor, pathetic girl again, who needed his strength because she had none of her own. 'And, more importantly, I'm not your responsibility.'

'Think again,' he said, trampling over her resistance, the muscle in his jaw now dancing a jig. 'Because until I sign those papers you're still my lawfully wedded wife.'

It was an insane thing to say. But much more insane was the stutter in her pulse, the fluttering sensation deep in her abdomen at the conviction in his voice.

'Don't be ridiculous, Dane. We are not *actually* married and we haven't been for over ten years. What we're talking about is an admin error that you wouldn't even know about if I hadn't come to see you today.'

'About that…' He hooked a tendril of hair behind her ear. 'Why *did* you come all the way to Manhattan when you could have gotten your attorney to handle it?'

It was a pertinent question—and one she didn't have a coherent answer for.

The rough pad of his fingertip trailed down her neck and into the hollow of her throat, sending sensation rioting across her collarbone and plunging into her breasts.

She should tell him to back off. She needed to leave. But something deeper and much more primal kept her immobile.

'You know what I think?' he said, his voice hoarse.

She shook her head. But she did know, and she really didn't want to.

'I think you missed me.'

'Don't be silly. I haven't thought of you in years,' she said, but the denial came out on a breathless whisper, convincing no one.

His lips lifted on one side, the don't-give-a-damn half-smile was an invitation to sin she'd never been able to resist.

'You don't remember how good it used to be between us?' he mocked, finding the punching pulse at the base of her throat. 'Because I do.'

His thumb rubbed back and forth across her collar-bone, the nonchalant caress incinerating the lacy fabric of her camisole.

'No,' she said, but they both knew that was the biggest lie of all.

A wad of something hard and immovable jammed her throat as his thumb drifted down to circle her nipple, the possessive, unapologetic touch electrifying even through the layers of silk and lace.

The peak engorged in a rush, poking against the fabric and announcing how big a whopper she'd told.

She needed to tell him to stop. He had no right to touch her like this any more. But the words refused to form as her back stretched, thrusting the rigid tip into his palm.

He dipped his head as his thumb traced the edge of her bra cup, rough calluses rasping sensitive skin as it slid beneath the lace. His lips nudged the corner of her mouth, so close she could smell coffee and peppermint.

'You were always a terrible liar, Red.'

She couldn't breathe. Couldn't think. Certainly couldn't speak.

So objecting was an impossibility when he eased the cup down to expose one tight nipple and blew on the sensitive flesh.

'Oh, God.'

Her lungs seized and her thigh muscles dissolved as he licked the tender peak, then nipped at the tip. She bucked, the shock of sensation bringing her hip into contact with the impressive ridge in his trousers. She rubbed against it like a cat, desperate to find relief from the exquisite agony.

He swore under his breath, then clasped her head and slanted his lips across hers. She opened for him instinctively and let his tongue plunder her mouth, driving the kiss into dark, torturous territory.

Her fingers curled into his shirt to drag him closer, absorbing his tantalising strength as the slab of muscle crushed her naked breast.

Her sex became heavy and painfully tender. Slick with longing. The melting sensation a throwback to her youth—when all he'd had to do was look at her to make her ready for him.

How can I still need him this much?

Her mind blurred, sinking into the glorious sex-fogged oblivion she'd denied herself for so long. *Too long.* Her tongue tangled with his, giving him the answer they both craved.

He kissed the way she remembered. With masterful thrusts and parries joined by teasing nips and licks as he devoured her mouth, no quarter given.

The day-old beard abraded her chin. Large hands brushed her thighs, bunching the skirt around her waist until he had a good firm grip on her backside.

Excitement pumped through her veins like a powerful narcotic, burning away everything but the sight, the sound, the scent of him.

He boosted her up—taking charge, taking control, the way she had always adored.

'Put your legs round my waist.'

She obeyed the husky command without question, clinging to his strong shoulders. Her heartbeat kicked her ribs and pummelled her sex as their tongues duelled, hot and wet and frantic.

Her back hit the wall with a thud and the thick ridge in his trousers ground against her panties, the friction exquisite against her yearning clitoris.

Holding her up with one arm, he tore at her underwear. The sound of ripping satin echoed off the room's hard surfaces, stunning her until he found her with his thumb. She moaned into his mouth, the perfect touch charging through her system like lightning.

His answering groan rumbled against her ear, harsh with need. 'Still so wet for me, Red?'

Blunt fingers brushed expertly over the heart of her, then circled the swollen nub, teasing, coaxing, demanding a response. Everything inside her drove down to that one tight spot, desperate to feel the touch which would drive her over. The coil tightened like a vice and propelled her mindlessly towards the peak.

'Please...' The single word came out on a tortured sob.

Dane was the only man who knew exactly what she needed and always had.

Suddenly he withdrew his fingers, sliding them through the wet folds to rest on her hip. Leaving her teetering on the edge of ecstasy.

She panted. Squirmed. Denied the touch she needed. The touch she had to have.

'Don't stop.'

He buried his face against her neck, the harsh pants of his breathing as tortured as her own. 'Have to,' he grunted.

'Why?'

Her dazed mind reeled, her flesh clenching painfully on emptiness. Desire clawed at her insides like a ravenous beast as he left her balanced brutally on the sharp edge between pleasure and pain.

'No *way* am I taking you without a condom.'

As the sex fog finally released its stranglehold on her brain the comment registered and horrifying reality smacked into her with the force and fury of an eighteen-wheeler. The nuclear blush mushroomed up to her hairline.

Did you actually just beg him to make love to you? Without protection?

If only there was such a thing as death by mortification.

This was now officially *the* most humiliating moment of her life. The trashy novel swoon had merely been a dress rehearsal.

She scooped her breast back into her bra, its reddened nipple mocking her.

She had to get away from here. Sod the divorce papers. She'd deal with them later. Right now saving herself and her sanity was more important than saving Carmichael's.

CHAPTER SIX

DANE BREATHED IN the sultry scent of Xanthe's arousal, still holding on to her butt as if she were the only solid object in the middle of a tornado.

How could it be exactly the same between them? The heat, the hunger, the insanity?

He felt as if he'd just been in a war. And he was fairly sure it was a war he hadn't won.

What were you thinking, hitting on her like that?

He'd been mad. Mad that he'd shouted at her, mad that she'd collapsed in front of him, and madder still that he cared enough about her to be sorry. But most of all he'd been mad that he could still want her so much, despite everything.

The come-on had been a ploy to intimidate her, to make her fold and do as she was told. But she hadn't. She'd met his demands with demands of her own. And suddenly they'd been racing to the point of no return like a couple of sex-mad teenagers—as if the last ten years had never happened.

'Dane, put me down. You're crushing me.'

The furious whisper brought him crashing the rest of the way back to reality.

He drew in an agonising breath of her scent. Light floral perfume and subtle sin. And lifted his head to survey the full extent of the damage.

Her hair had tumbled down, sticking in damp strands to the line of her throat. A smudge of mascara added to the bluish tinge under her eyes, the reddened skin on her chin and cheek suggesting she was going to have some serious beard-burn in the morning.

He should have shaved. Then again, he should have done a lot of things.

She looked shell-shocked.

He had the weird urge to laugh. At least he wasn't the only one.

She pushed against his chest, struggling to get out of his arms in earnest.

'Stop staring at me like that. I have to leave.'

He let her go and watched her scramble away, trying to be grateful that he'd at least managed to stop himself from leaping off the deep end this time. The painful erection made sure he didn't feel nearly as great about that last-minute bout of sanity as he should.

She swept her hair back and bent to slip on the heels which must have fallen off at some point during their sex apocalypse, making it impossible for him not to notice how the slim skirt highlighted the generous contours of her butt. He tore his gaze away.

Haven't you tortured yourself enough already?

She pressed a hand to her forehead, glancing round—

still struggling to calm down, to take stock and figure out what the heck had just happened was his guess.

Good luck with that.

'I should go.' She smoothed her clothing with unsteady hands and brushed a wayward curl behind her ear. It sprang straight back.

He planted his hands in his pants pockets and resisted the urge to hook it back round her ear a second time. Because look how that had ended the first time.

She was right. She should go. Before the urge to follow through on what they'd just started got the better of them.

Hitting on her had been a dumb move. What exactly had he been trying to prove? That she still wanted him? That he was the one in charge? Or just that he was the biggest dumbass on the planet?

Because, whatever way you looked at it, that dumb move had stirred up stuff neither one of them was ready to deal with. Yet.

'You think?' he sneered, because their sex apocalypse wasn't just on *him*.

She'd made the decision to sneak back into his life and poke at something that had died a long time ago. And when he'd made that first dumb move, instead of telling him no she'd gone off like a rocket—giving him a taste of the girl he remembered which he wasn't going to be able to forget any time soon.

She glared at him, picking up on his pissy tone.

Yeah, that's right, sweetheart. I'm the guy you decided wasn't good enough for you. The guy you still can't get enough of.

'Don't you dare try to put this insanity on *me*,' she said.

'I didn't start it. And, anyway, we finished it before things got totally out of hand. So it's not important.'

Hell, yeah, it is. If I say it is.

'*We* didn't finish it,' he pointed out, because scoring a direct hit seemed vitally important. '*I* did.'

The flush scorched her skin and she blew out a staggered breath. 'So what? I got a little carried away in the heat of the moment. That's all.'

'A *little*?' Talk about an understatement.

Her lips set in a mulish line, the blush still beaming on those beard-scorched cheeks.

'It was a mistake, okay? Brought on by stress and fatigue and...' She paused, her gaze darting pretty much everywhere but his face. 'And sexual deprivation.'

'Sexual deprivation?' He scoffed. 'How do you figure *that*?'

She was going to have to spell that one out for him.

'I've been extremely busy for the past five years. Obviously I needed to blow off some steam.'

He should have been insulted. And a part of him was. But a much larger part of him wanted to know if she'd really just told him she'd been celibate for five years.

'Exactly how long has it been since you got to "blow off some steam"?'

Her eyes narrowed. 'That's none of your business.'

'That long, huh?' he mocked, enjoying the spark of temper—and the news that he'd been her first in a while—probably way too much.

He'd never sparred with her when she was a girl. Because she'd always been too cute and too fragile. It would have been like kicking a puppy. He'd always had to be so careful, mindful of how delicate she was. Back then he'd been terrified he'd break her, that his rough, low-class hands would be too demanding for all that delicate, petal-soft skin. So he'd strived hard to be gentle even when it had cost him.

But she'd given as good as she'd gotten a minute ago. And damn if that didn't turn him on even more.

The flush now mottled the skin of her cleavage, and suddenly he was remembering gliding his tongue across her nipple, her soft sob of encouragement as he captured the hard bud between his teeth.

His blood surged south. And he got mad all over again.

She'd been so far out of his reach that summer. But somehow she'd hooked him into her drama, her reality, made him want to stand up to her daddy, to fight her demons, to brand her as his and follow some cock-eyed dream. When she'd told him she was pregnant he'd been horrified at first, but much worse had been the driving need that had opened up inside him—the fierce desire to claim her and their child.

She'd convinced him she wanted to keep his baby. And that was all it had taken to finally tip him over into an alternative reality where he'd kidded himself they could make it work. That she really wanted to make it work. With him. A British heiress and a nobody from Roxbury. *As if.*

He'd spent years afterwards dealing with her betrayal, determined that no one would ever have the power to screw him over like that again—even after he'd finally figured out that she'd probably just been playing him all along so she could stick it to her overbearing daddy.

The thought that he could still want her so much infuriated the hell out of him. But he'd just behaved like a wild man, making it tough to deny.

He'd ripped off her panties, damn it. When was the last time he'd done something like *that*? Been so desperate to get to a woman he'd torn off her underwear? Hadn't even taken the time or trouble to undress her properly, to kiss her and caress her?

He might not be a master of small talk, but he had some moves. Moves women generally appreciated and which he'd worked at acquiring over the last ten years.

Until Xanthe had strolled back into his life and managed to rip away all those layers of class and sophistication and bring back that rough, raw, reckless, screwed-up kid. The kid he'd always hated.

She made a dash for the elevators.

'Hey, wait up!' He chased her down, grabbed her wrist.

She swung round, her eyes bright with fury and panic. 'Don't touch me. I'm not staying.'

He lifted his hand away. 'I get that. But I want to know where you're going.' He scrambled for a plausible reason. 'So I can get the papers delivered tomorrow.'

In person.

'You'll sign them?'

She sounded so surprised and so relieved he wondered if there was more to those papers than she was letting on. Because she *had* to know there was no way on earth he would want to contest their divorce—no matter how hot they still were for each other.

Focus, dumbass.

He shook off the suspicion. His objective right now was to make sure she didn't hightail it all the way back to London before he was finished with her.

This wasn't over. Not by a long shot. But he'd learned the hard way that it was better to retreat and work out a strategy rather than risk riding roughshod straight into an ambush.

Her old man and his goons had taught him that on the night he'd come to collect his wife—believing he had rights and obligations only to discover that promises meant nothing if you were rich and privileged and already over the piece of trash you'd married.

The anger surged back, fresh and vivid, but he was ready for it now, in a way he hadn't been earlier.

So had he been kidding himself that he was over what she'd done? That didn't have to be bad. As long as he dealt with it once and for all.

'Sure, I'll sign them,' he replied.

Once I'm good and ready.

She'd stirred up this hornets' nest, so he wasn't going to be the only one who got stung.

'Thank you,' she said, and the stunned pleasure in her voice crucified him a little. 'I'm glad we finally got the chance to end this properly. I didn't have—' She stopped abruptly, cutting off the thought, her cheeks heating.

'You didn't have what?'

What had she been about to say? Because whatever it was she looked stricken that she'd almost let it slip.

'Nothing.'

Yeah, right. Then why was her guilty flush bright enough to signal incoming aircraft?

'I hope we can part as friends,' she said, thrusting her hand out like a peace offering, the long slim fingers visibly shaking.

Friends, my butt.

They weren't friends. Or their marriage would not have ended the way it had. Friends were honest with each other. Friends were people you could trust. And when had he ever been able to trust *her*?

But still he clasped her hand, and squeezed gently to stem the tremor.

She let go first, tugging free to press the elevator button. She stepped into the car when it arrived, her eyes downcast. But as she turned to hit the lobby button their gazes met.

The muscle under his heart clenched.

'Goodbye, Dane.'

He nodded as the doors slid shut. Then he pulled out his mobile and dialled his PA.

'Mel? Ms Carmichael—' he paused '—I mean Ms Sanders, whose real name is Carmichael, is going to be stopping by any second to collect her briefcase. I want you to book her a suite at The Standard for the night and bill it to me. Then arrange a car to take her there.'

The place was classy, and only a few blocks away on the High Line. He wanted to know exactly where she was.

He didn't want any more nasty surprises. From here on in this was his game and his rules. And he was playing to win.

'Okay,' Mel said, sounding confused but, like the excellent assistant she was, not questioning his authority. Unlike his soon-to-be ex-wife. 'Is there anything else?'

'Yeah, if she kicks up a fuss…' He wouldn't put it past the new, improved kick-ass Xanthe to do the one thing guaranteed to screw up his plans. 'Tell her taking care of her accommodation is the least I could do…' He paused, the lie that would ensure Xanthe accepted his offer tasting bittersweet. 'For a *friend.*'

CHAPTER SEVEN

THAT EVENING XANTHE stood in front of the bathroom mirror in the corner suite her ex-husband had booked for her as a final gesture of 'friendship,' still trying to feel good about the outcome of their forced trip down memory lane that afternoon.

Tomorrow morning she would have the signed divorce papers in her hand, all threats to Carmichael's would be gone, and she and Dane could both get back to their lives as if Augustus Greaves and his shoddy workmanship had never happened.

Mission accomplished.

The only problem was she didn't feel good about what had happened in Dane's office and later in his apartment. She felt edgy and tense and vaguely guilty— thoughts and emotions still colliding in her brain three hours later, like a troop of toddlers on a sugar rush.

She smoothed aloe vera moisturiser over the red skin on her face which, fresh from a long hot bath loaded with the hotel's luxury bath salts, beamed like a stop light. If only she'd seen that warning before she'd let Dane devour her, because stubble rash was the least of her worries.

The memory of his rough, frantic handling sent an unwelcome shiver of awareness through her exhausted body. Firm, sensual lips subjugating hers, that marauding tongue plunging deep and obliterating all rational thought, solid pecs rippling beneath her grasping fingers, his teeth biting into her bottom lip and sending need arrowing down to her core...

She gripped the sink, her thighs turning to mush. *Again.*

She shivered, even though the bathroom's central air was set at the perfect ambient temperature. She needed to sleep. And forget about this afternoon's events.

But sleep continued to elude her.

She'd had some success in distracting herself for the first hour after Dane's driver had deposited her at the striking modernist hotel on Manhattan's High Line Park by doing what she did best—formulating an extensive to-do list and then doing it to death.

The first order of business had been to book herself on the evening flight to Heathrow tomorrow and bump herself up to first class. After today's 'episode' a lie-flat seat was going to be a necessity.

With her flight booked, she'd messed around for another thirty minutes selecting designer jeans, a fashionable T-shirt, fresh underwear and a pair of flats online from a nearby boutique and getting a guarantee that it would be express-delivered by tomorrow morning at 10 a.m. No matter how washed out she felt, at least she wouldn't have to *look* washed out, wearing her creased silk suit on the flight home.

Unfortunately while actioning her to-do list she'd

got a second wind that she didn't seem able to shake—even after soaking for twenty minutes in the suite's enormous bathtub.

She just wanted to turn her brain off now and get comatose. But she couldn't. Maybe it was the jet lag kicking in? It was close to dawn now in the UK—the time she usually woke up to get ready for work and have her morning caffeine hit while sitting on the balcony of her luxury flat by the River Thames, allowing herself five minutes to enjoy the sun rising over Tower Bridge.

Her body clock had obviously decided that habit wasn't going to change, no matter what time zone she was in. Or how shattered she felt.

Unfortunately, being unable to sleep had given her far too much time to dissect all the things that had gone wrong this afternoon. Her fainting fit, the shocking revelation that Dane had assumed she'd aborted their child, but most of all her ludicrous reaction to Dane's come-on.

And she'd come to one irrefutable conclusion. When she got back to London she needed to look at options to get back in the dating game—because all work and no sex had clearly turned her into an unexploded bomb. She hadn't had a date in three years, no actual intimate contact in at least four, and she hadn't gone all the way since...

Xanthe watched the frown puckering her brow in the mirror deepen into a crevice.

Since the last time she'd made love to Dane.

No wonder she'd lost it with him. Her physical reaction to him had nothing to do with their past—or any lingering feelings—and everything to do with her failure to find another man with the same orgasm-on-demand capabilities as her ex-husband.

Since Dane, she'd always taken care of her own orgasms. At first she had put it down to some kind of perverse physical loyalty to the man who had abandoned her. Whenever another man touched her, her body had insisted on comparing him to Dane. Her failure to get aroused hadn't bothered her too much—in fact she'd begun to think it was a boon. After all, she never wanted to be a slave to her sex drive again—so in thrall to a guy's sexual prowess that she confused lust with love.

But apparently her sex drive was still a slave to *Dane's* sexual prowess.

Don't go there. It doesn't mean anything.

Dane wasn't unique. He didn't have some special mojo that made her more susceptible, more in tune to his touch than to any other guy's. She just hadn't found the right guy yet—the right 'other guy' to hit all her happy buttons—because she hadn't been looking.

She'd got so used to taking care of her own business the loss hadn't become apparent until she'd walked into Dane's office this afternoon and had some kind of sexual breakdown. Triggered by Dane, who—in his usual in-your-face style—had decided to demonstrate exactly what she had been missing.

Of course she'd responded to Dane with all the restraint of a firecracker meeting a naked flame. She'd been running on stress and adrenaline for three days, and working herself to the bone for a great deal longer.

Dane had always known how to trip her switch, how

to touch and caress and take her in ways that gave her no choice but to respond. And that obviously hadn't changed. But only because she'd been holding herself hostage for ten years...not exploring the possibilities.

After the trauma of their marriage, she had convinced herself in the last ten years that an active and fulfilled sex-life wasn't important. But clearly it *was* important—to her sense of self and her sense of well-being.

When she got back to the UK she was going to remedy that. Why not check out a few dating websites?

She shuddered involuntarily.

But until then she needed to get rid of all the sexual energy pumping around her system and stopping her from dropping into the exhausted sleep she so desperately needed.

She touched her fingertip to the tender skin on her chin, then trailed the nail down, inadvertently following the path Dane had taken three hours ago. Parting her robe, she sucked in a breath as the cool satin brushed over the tender skin of her nipple. Hooking the lapel round her breast to expose herself, she circled the ripe areola, still supremely sensitive from Dane's attentions. Her nipple rose in ruched splendour, the air cool against heated flesh. The gush of response between her thighs settled low in her abdomen, warm and fluid and heavy. She pinched the nipple, remembering the sharp nip of his teeth, and the coil of need tightened into a knot.

Untying the robe's belt, she let it fall open, revealing the neatly trimmed curls at the apex of her thighs, and spotted a small bruise on her hip. She ran her finger over the mark, remembering the feel of Dane's fingers digging into her skin as he boosted her into his arms.

'Wrap your legs round my waist.'

She cupped her aching sex, pressing the heel of her palm hard against her pelvic bone.

But as she closed her eyes all she could see was Dane's eyes staring back at her, the iridescent blue of the irises almost invisible round the lust-blown pupils, the hot look demanding she come…but only for him.

She parted the wet folds, but as she ran the pad of her finger over the tight bundle of nerves all she could feel were the urgent flicks and caresses of thick, blunt, calloused fingers.

'Always so damn wet for me, Red.'

His low, husky voice reverberated through her as she rubbed her clitoris in urgent, helpless strokes. She knew the right touch, the perfect touch to take her over quickly and efficiently. But this time the memory of Dane's fingers, firm and sure, mocked her battle for release, teasing and tempting her, taking her higher, and higher.

She panted. Not quite there yet. Never. Quite. There.

'Please, please…'

She slammed her palm down on the vanity unit and opened her eyes to see a mad woman staring back at her—hot, bothered and still hopelessly frustrated.

Every nerve-ending pulsated, desperate for release. A release that remained resolutely out of reach. Tantalising her senses…torturing her already-battered brain. A release she was very much afraid only Dane could give her.

The bastard.

Damn her ex-husband. Had he ruined her now for herself? As well as for every other man? How was that fair? Or proportionate?

She tied the robe with shaking hands, covering her nakedness. The flushed skin was screaming in protest, too sensitive now even for the silky feel of satin. She washed her hands and swallowed round the fireball in her throat, which was equal parts mortification and arousal. Cursing Dane and his clever, commanding caresses with every staggered breath.

She walked back into the bedroom of the suite and crossed to the phone. She would call down and ask for some sleeping pills. She hated taking any kind of medication, hated having her senses dulled, but if she didn't do something soon the toddlers in her head were liable to explode right out of her ears.

Whatever black magic Dane had worked on her sex-starved body this afternoon would be undone by a decent ten hours' sleep, and tomorrow evening she would be winging her way back across the Atlantic, the signed papers snug in her briefcase.

She was never going to see him again. Or feel his knowing fingers. Or watch his sexy I'm-gonna-make-you-come-like-an-express-train smile. And that was exactly how she wanted it. She was her own woman now. Or she would be again, once she was out of his line of fire.

A sharp rap at the door had her hesitating as she lifted the handset.

It took her tired mind a moment to process the interruption, but then she remembered. Her clothes. In typically efficient New York City style, the boutique had delivered them ahead of schedule.

Dropping the phone she crossed the room and flung open the door without bothering to check the peephole.

All the blood drained out of her head and raced down to pound in her already pouting clitoris. And the toddlers in her head began mainlining cocaine.

'Dane, what are you doing here?'

And why do you have to look so incredible?

Her ex stood on the threshold in worn jeans and a long-sleeved blue T-shirt covered by a chequered shirt. The buzz cut shone black in the light from the hallway, complementing the dark frown on his handsome face. Wisps of chest hair revealed by the T-shirt's V-neck announced his overwhelming masculinity. Not that it needed any more of an introduction.

With his broad shoulders blocking the doorway, his imposing height towering over her own five feet six inches in her bare feet and his blue eyes glittering with intent, he looked even more capable of leaping tall buildings in a single bound in casual clothing than he had in his captain of industry outfit.

'We need to talk.'

Flattening a large hand against the door, he pushed it open and strolled past her into the room before she could object.

'We've already talked,' she said, her voice as unsteady as her heartbeat as she gripped the lapels of the flimsy robe, drawing them over her throat in a vain attempt to hide at least some of the marks left by his kisses.

She squeezed her traitorous nipples under folded forearms to alleviate the sudden rush of blood which had them standing out against the satin-like torpedoes ready to launch.

Good grief, she was as good as naked, while he was fully dressed. No wonder her heartbeat was punching her pulse points with the force of a heavyweight champ.

He turned, his size even more intimidating than usual as he stepped close. *Too close*. She took a step back, not caring if it made her look weak. Right now she *felt* weak. Too weak to resist her physical reaction to him. And that would be bad for a number of reasons. None of which she could recall, because her brain was packed full of cotton wool and rampaging toddlers tripping on cocaine.

'You shouldn't be here,' she said, wanting to mean it.

'What didn't you have?'

The terse question had the toddlers hitting a brick wall while the endorphin rush detonated into a thousand fragments of shrapnel.

'Excuse me?'

'You said, "I didn't have," and then you stopped. What were you about to say?'

'I have no idea.'

'You're lying.' Dane could see it in her eyes. The translucent blue-green was alive with anxiety as her teeth trapped her bottom lip.

Unfortunately he could also see she was naked under her robe. And his body was already riding roughshod over all sensible thought.

Blood charged into his groin, but he kept his gaze steady on hers. He'd spent the last three hours trying to convince himself that seeing her again would be nuts. Why not just sign the divorce papers, have Mel deliver them tomorrow and put an end to this whole fiasco?

But that one half-sentence, that one phrase that she'd left hanging kept coming back to torment him. That and the brutal heat that he had begun to realise had never died.

'I didn't have...'

Eventually he'd been unable to stand it any more. So he'd walked the three blocks to the hotel. There was something she wasn't telling him. And that something was something he needed to know.

Maybe they meant nothing to each other now. But they had once, and not all his feelings had faded the way they should have. Which might explain why his libido hadn't got the memo.

He still wanted her, and it was driving him crazy.

The light perfume of her scent, the sight of her hair curling in damp strands to her shoulders, the moist patches making the wet satin cling to her collarbone, the trembling fingers closing the robe while he imagined all the treasures that lay beneath...

Damn it, Redmond. Concentrate. You're not here to jump her. You're here to get the truth.

He'd convinced himself that she'd got rid of their kid because she'd *had* to, because it had been the only way she could be shot of him, and he'd never questioned it, but in the last three hours he'd begun picking apart the evidence—and not one bit of it made any sense.

He'd always known Xanthe didn't love him, because no one *really* loved anyone else. But when had she ever given him any indication that she didn't want to keep their baby? Never. Not once. She had been the one who had insisted she wanted to have it when the stick had turned blue. She had been the one to say yes instantly when he'd suggested marriage. She had been the one who had kept on smiling every morning as she'd puked her guts up in the motel bathroom while he was left feeling tense and scared. And she'd been the one who had never stopped talking about the tiny life inside her. So much so, that she'd made him believe in it, too.

How could that girl have given up on their baby because of one dumb argument?

'I'm not lying,' she said. 'And you need to leave.'

The quiver of distress in her voice made a mockery of the spark of defiance in her eyes. He could see the war she was waging to stay strong and immune. Her back was ramrod-straight, and her chin stuck out as if she were waiting for him to take a shot at it.

Frustration tangled with lust.

Gripping her upper arms, he tugged her towards him. Her muscles tensed under his palms, the thin layer of smooth satin over warm skin sending sex messages to his brain he did not need.

'Tell me the truth, Red. What really happened to our baby? You owe me that much.'

A shudder ran through her and she looked away— but not before he spotted the flare of anguish.

'Please don't do this. None of it matters any more.'

'It does to me,' he said, and the feelings inside him—

feelings he'd thought he'd conquered years ago—raced out of hiding to sucker-punch him all over again.

Hurt, loss, sadness, but most of all that futile festering rage.

Except this time the rage wasn't directed at Xanthe but at himself. Why hadn't he fought harder to see her? Why hadn't he made more of an effort to get past her father and his goons and find out what had really happened?

She kept her head down, but a lone tear trickled down the side of her face. Pain stabbed into his gut—a dull echo of the pain when Carmichael's goons had dragged him off the estate and beaten him until he'd been unable to fight back.

'Look at me, Xan.'

She gave a loud sniff and shook her head.

Cradling her cheek, he brushed the tear away with his thumb and raised her face to his. Her eyes widened, shadowed with hopelessness and grief, glittering with unshed tears.

And suddenly he knew. The truth he should have figured out ten years ago. The truth that would have been obvious to him then if he'd been less of a screwed-up, insecure kid and more of a man.

He swore softly and folded his arms around her, trying to absorb the pain.

'You didn't have an abortion, did you?'

He said the words against her hair, breathing in the clean scent of lemon verbena, anchoring her fragile frame against his much stronger one.

His emotions tangled into a gut-wrenching mix of

anger and pain and guilt. How could he have got things so wrong? And what did he do with the information now?

She stood rigid in his arms, refusing to soften, refusing to take the comfort he offered. The comfort her old man had denied them both.

He swallowed down the ache in his throat. 'That sucks, Red.'

She drew in a deep, fortifying breath, her whole body starting to shake like a leaf in a hurricane. He tightened his arms, feeling helpless and inadequate but knowing, this once, that he was not going to take the easy road. She wasn't that girl any more—sweet and sunny and stupidly in love with a guy who had never existed—and up until two seconds ago he would have thought he was glad of it. But now he wasn't so sure.

His throat burned as she trembled in his arms and he mourned the loss of that bright, optimistic girl who had always believed the best of him when he had been unable to believe it himself.

CHAPTER EIGHT

'I'M SO SORRY, Mrs Redmond. There's no heartbeat and we need to operate to stop the bleeding.'

The storm of emotion raged inside her, the sobs she'd repressed for so long choking her as her mind dragged her back to that darkest of dark days. Lying on the hospital gurney, the white-suited doctor looking down at her with pity in his warm brown eyes…

Dane's hand stroked her hair. His heartbeat felt strong and steady through worn cotton, his chest solid, immovable, offering her the strength she'd needed then and been so cruelly denied. Tearing pain racked her body as she remembered how alone, how useless, how helpless she'd felt that day. And the horror that had followed.

She gulped for air, her arms yearning to cling to his strength as tears she couldn't afford to shed made her throat close.

Be strong. Don't cry. Don't you dare break.

He kissed her hair, murmuring reassurances, apologies that she'd needed so badly then but refused to need now. Then his hips butted hers and she felt the potent outline of him, semihard against her belly.

Arousal surged in her shattered body, thick and sure and so simple. Reaction shuddered down to her core.

Flattening her hands against the tense muscles of his belly, she pushed out of his arms and looked up to find him watching her, his expression grim with regret and yet tight with arousal. Reaching up, she ran her palms over his hair, the way she'd wanted to do as soon as she'd walked into his office.

Absorbing the delicious tingle of the short bristles against her skin, she framed his face and dragged his mouth down to hers. 'You're ten years too late, Dane. There's only one thing I want now.'

Or only one thing she could still allow herself to take.

His eyes flared and her body rejoiced. This was the one thing they had always been good at. She didn't want his pity, his regret, his sympathy—all she wanted was to feel that glorious heat pounding into her and making her forget about the pain.

His mouth captured hers, his tongue plunging deep, demanding entry. She opened for him, the heady thrill obliterating the treacherous memories.

Large hands ran up her sides under the robe, rough calluses against soft skin bringing her body to shimmering life. He crushed her against him, banding strong arms around her back, forcing her soft curves to yield to his strength. She draped her arms over his shoulders as he picked her up, carried her to the king-sized bed and dropped her into the centre. Parting the thin satin with impatient hands, he swept his burning gaze over her naked skin, the dark rapture in his eyes making her feel like a sacrifice already burning at the stake.

She reached for his belt, desperate to wrap her fingers round his thick length and make him melt, too. But he gripped her wrists and pinned her hands to the mattress above her head, leaving her naked and exposed while he was still fully clothed.

'Not yet,' he growled, the barely leashed demand in his gruff voice exciting in its intensity. 'Let me touch you first. Or this is gonna last about two seconds.'

She stopped struggling against his hold, the terse admission more gratifying than a thousand declarations of undying devotion. Lying boneless, she let her own hunger overwhelm her, frantic to feel the rush of release that would make her forget everything but this day, this hour, this moment.

It was madness, but it was divine madness—the perfect end to a disastrous day. She was sick of thinking about consequences, about her own troubled emotions and the implications of everything that had happened ten years ago. She was sick of thinking, full stop. And, however else Dane had failed her—as a husband, as a friend—he had never failed her as a lover.

Still holding her wrists, he bent to kiss her lips, his mouth firm and demanding, before trailing kisses down her neck, across her collarbone. She rose off the bed, his groan a potent aphrodisiac as he licked at one pouting nipple.

A soft sob escaped her as he ran his tongue around the areola and then suckled the hard bud, making it swell against his lips into a bullet of need. She moaned, low and deep, as he bit into the tender flesh. Hunger arrowed down to her core. Sharp and sure and unstoppable. And then he transferred his attentions to the other breast.

She panted, writhing under the sensual torture. 'Please, I need you...'

'I know what you need, baby,' he growled. 'Open your eyes.'

She did as he demanded, to find his striking blue gaze locked on hers. Bracketing her wrists in one restraining hand, he watched her as he found her wet and wanting. She lifted her hips, pushing into the unbearably light caress as the moisture released.

She couldn't think, couldn't feel, her skin burned as his playful strokes had the pleasure swelling and then retreating, tempting and then denying.

'Dane...' His name came out on a broken cry. 'Stop messing about.'

He barked out a harsh laugh, the fierce arousal in his face sending her senses into overdrive. 'You want me to use my superpower?'

'You know I do. You...'

Her angry words dissolved in a loud moan as he released her wrists to part her legs. Holding her open with his thumbs, he blew across the heated flesh. She bucked off the bed. The tiny contact unbearable.

She watched, transfixed, shaking with desire as his dark head bent and his tongue began to explore her slick folds. A thin, desperate cry tore from her throat as blunt fingers entered her, first one, then two, stretching her, torturing that hotspot deep inside only he knew would throw her over the edge.

She screamed, her fingers digging into his hair, urging him on as he set his mouth on her at last, suckling the swollen nub. She hurtled into glorious oblivion, exquisite rapture slamming into her as her senses exploded into a thousand shards of glittering light.

Dane lifted himself up, the lingering taste of her sweet and succulent, the need for release unbearable. She stared at him, her eyes wide, the sea-green dazed and wary, her body flushed with pleasure, her skin luminous.

Damn, but she was the most beautiful woman he'd ever seen. Even more beautiful than before. She'd lost that openness, that faith in him that had always scared the hell out of him, and now she had a million secrets of her own, but he could still zap her with his superpower.

The old joke made him smile—but the smile turned to a grimace as the insistent throbbing in his groin tipped from torment into torture.

If he didn't get inside her in the next two seconds he was liable to embarrass himself.

Dane located the condoms in the front pocket of his jeans and grappled with his belt and shoved his pants down. He ripped open a foil packet and rolled on the protection. Grasping her hips, he lifted her up, then paused.

'Tell me you want this.'

Tell me you want me.

The pathetic plea echoed in his head and made him tense. This was about sex and chemistry, pure and simple. Raw, rough, elemental. He didn't need her approval. He just needed to be inside her.

'You know I do,' she said, bold and defiant.

He stopped thinking and plunged deep, burying himself to the hilt, then groaned, struggling to give her time to adjust before he began to move.

'You okay? You're so tight...' His mind reeled, remembering it had been a while for her. Five years at least. His heady sense of victory at the thought was almost as insane as the delirious wish to be able to take her without a condom.

Draping her arms over his shoulders, she lifted herself up to angle her hips and take him deeper. 'Just move.'

'Yes, ma'am,' he said, laughing.

She was his. She had always been his in the only way that really meant anything.

He drew out, thrust back, feeling her clench around him. The heat in his abdomen built into an inferno as he established a ruthless rhythm, determined to drive her over again before he found his own release.

He clung on to control, an explosive orgasm licking at the base of his spine as her soft sobs became hoarse cries and she reached the point of no return. Her muscles clamped tight, massaging his length as she hit her peak. He thrust once, twice, and collapsed on top of her, his brutal release violent in its intensity as his seed exploded into the sweet, shuddering clasp of her body.

CHAPTER NINE

'WELL, THAT WAS...' Xanthe struggled to breathe while being crushed into the mattress, the floaty, fluffy sensation fading fast to be replaced with all the aches and pains of not one but two mind-blowing orgasms.

Her brain knotted with the stupidity of what they'd just done.

He shifted, lifting his weight from her, and the sensual smile on his too-handsome face was both arrogant and strangely endearing.

'Awesome,' he supplied.

'Actually, I was going to say insane.'

He grunted out a strained laugh and rolled off her. Xanthe watched him sitting on the edge of the bed with his back to her as he bent to untie his boots and then kick his pants off the rest of the way.

'More like inevitable.' He took off his shirt and balled it up to drop it next to his jeans. 'Since we've both been primed for it since this afternoon,' he added, his voice muffled as he pulled his T-shirt over his head and dumped it on the pile of clothing.

Her throat clogged at the sight of his broad back,

deeply tanned but for the whiter strip of skin on his backside and the now faded scars that stood out in criss-crossing stripes across his ribs. An echo of sympathy and sorrow and curiosity about those marks hit her unawares. She forced the feelings down, disturbed by the direction of her thoughts.

Dane's secrets were his own and always had been, and they were no concern of hers.

He stood up and strolled across the room, gloriously naked, his languid stride both arrogant and unashamed. Xanthe became transfixed by the bunch and flex of the gluteal muscles in his tight, beautifully sculpted butt cheeks. Her body hummed back to life—like one of those relighting candles people put on a birthday cake as a joke, with a flame that keeps flaring no matter how hard you try to blow it out.

She slipped under the sheets, far too aware of her own nakedness now. She'd always thought those candles were really annoying.

'What do you think you're doing?' she ventured, trying to sound stern.

He glanced back over one broad shoulder as he opened the bathroom door. 'Grabbing a shower.'

She hauled the sheet to her neckline to cover any hint of vulnerability. 'I don't remember inviting you to stay.'

He leaned against the door, thankfully shielding at least some of his more impressive assets and sent her a stern look that she suspected was much more effective than her own.

'I'm having a shower and then we're going to get to that talk.'

'I don't want to talk.' She ignored the raised eyebrow. 'All I want to do is sleep,' she protested.

And try to forget about the fact that Dane's position as her go-to guy for earth-shattering orgasms had not diminished in the least.

'Preferably alone,' she added for good measure.

Now that stallion had bolted out of the stable. Twice. She did not need a repeat performance.

'And you can,' he said. 'Once we're finished talking.'

'But...'

The door slammed behind him.

'I don't want you here,' she finished lamely as the power shower was switched on behind the closed door.

Oh, for—she swore, using a word that would have had Nanny Foster reaching for the soap.

The man was incorrigible. Domineering and dictatorial and completely contrary. Surely there could be nothing left to say about what had happened ten years ago? He'd figured out the truth, they'd jumped each other, had multi-orgasmic make-up sex...end of story.

If she were at full strength she would pick up the phone right now and call hotel security to have him thrown out. Even if it *would* be somewhat problematic explaining why they should be kicking out the man whose credit card details were on the room.

Unfortunately, though, she wasn't at full strength. She dragged her weary body out of the bed. If nothing else, the make-up sex had killed her second wind stone dead. She could happily sleep for a month now.

So she'd just have to go for damage limitation.

Grabbing a bunch of cushions off the sofa, she jammed them into the middle of the bed in case he got any ideas about joining her once he'd finished his shower.

And just in case *she* got any ideas…

She whisked his discarded T-shirt off the floor as the only nightwear option on offer—the hotel's satin robe had been about as useful as a negligee in a rugby scrum—and put it on to establish a second line of defence. The shirt hung down to mid-thigh, the sleeves covering her hands, and looked less enticing than a potato sack. Perfect.

Not so perfectly, it smelled of him—that far too enticing combination of washing powder and man.

She hauled herself back into the bed, trying not to notice the sexy scent as she prepared to stay awake for a few minutes more in order to give Dane his marching orders. Curling into a tight ball with her back to the wall of cushions, she watched the winking lights across the Hudson River through the hotel's floor-to-ceiling glass walls, and stared at the corner suite's awe-inspiring view of the Jersey shoreline.

The buzz of awareness subsided into a relaxing hum and the tender spot between her thighs became pleasantly numb. She inhaled his scent, lulled by the sound of running water from the shower.

The thundering beat of her heart slowed as her mind began to drift. Her eyelids drooped as she floated into dreams of hot, hazy days on the water and muscular arms holding her close and promising to keep her safe.

For ever.

* * *

Dane sat in his shorts and concentrated on finishing off the last few bites of the burger and fries he'd ordered from room service, mindful of the soft snores still coming from the pile of bedclothes a few feet away.

What was he still doing here?

Xanthe had been dead to the world ever since he'd come out of the bathroom. He'd thought at first she might be faking sleep to avoid the conversation they still needed to have about why she'd lied to him in his apartment. Letting him believe she had terminated the pregnancy. Why the heck hadn't she just told him about the miscarriage then, instead of waiting for him to figure it out on his own?

But after ten minutes of watching her sleep, her slim body curled in the bed like a child and barely moving, he'd conceded that not only wasn't she faking it, but she wasn't likely to stir until morning.

Given that, he had no business hanging around. They weren't a couple. And he didn't much like hanging around after sex even when the woman he'd just had sex with was a casual date, let alone his almost-ex-wife.

But once he'd begun to get dressed he'd been unable to locate his T-shirt. After hunting for a good ten minutes, he'd finally spotted a blue cuff peeking out from under the bedclothes. A quick inspection under the covers had been enough to locate the missing shirt—and trigger a series of unwanted memories.

Xanthe in her wet swimsuit on the deck of the pocket cruiser, pulling on his old high school sweatshirt to ward off the chill after a make-out session in the water. Him grabbing one of his work shirts to throw over her as she raced ahead of him into the motel bathroom, her belly rebelling in pregnancy. And a boatload of other equally vivid memories—some mercilessly erotic, others painfully poignant.

That old feeling of protectiveness had struck him hard in the chest—and stopped him from walking out.

He'd messed up ten years ago. She was right. He hadn't been there when she needed him. But there was nothing he could do about that now. Except apologise, and she hadn't wanted his apology.

He knew a damn distraction technique when he saw one, and that was what she'd done—used sex and chemistry as a means of keeping conversation at a minimum.

He'd been mad about that once he'd figured it out in the shower, but he'd calmed down enough now to see the irony. After all, mind-blowing sex had always been *his* go-to distraction technique when they were kids together and she'd asked him probing questions about the humiliating scars on his back.

Dumping the last of the burger on the plate, he covered the remains of the meal with the silver hood and wheeled the room service trolley into the hall.

Uneasiness settled over him as he returned to the suite. He needed to leave. She could keep the undershirt. He had a hundred others just like it. He didn't even know what he was still doing here.

But as he approached the bed to grab his work shirt off the floor and finish getting dressed a muffled sob rose from the lump of bedclothes, followed by a whimper of distress.

Edging the cover down, he looked at her face devoid of make-up, fresh and innocent, like the girl he remembered. But then her brow puckered, her lips drew tight, and her hand curled into a tight fist on the pillow beside her head. Rapid movement under her eyelids suggested she was having some kind of nightmare as she stifled another sob.

His heart punched his ribcage and got wedged in his throat. He needed to go. But instead of heading for the door he crouched beside the bed and rested his palm on her hair. He brushed the wild curling mass back from her forehead, instinct overriding common sense.

'Shh, Red, everything's okay. Go back to sleep.'

She shook off his hand, her breathing accelerating as the nightmare gripped her. 'Please pick up the phone Dane... *Please.*'

The hoarse, terrified whimpers tore at his conscience, guilt striking him unawares. Awake, she'd been strong and resilient. But asleep was another matter.

He couldn't walk away. Not yet.

Tugging on his jeans and leaving the top button undone, he whipped back the sheets to discover a row of cushions from the couch laid out down the middle of the bed. A rueful smile tugged at his mouth.

What was the great wall of throw pillows supposed to keep in check? His libido or hers?

Digging the makeshift barrier out of the bed, he slung the cushions back on the couch. Climbing in behind her, he gathered her shaking body into his arms until her back lay snug against his chest, her bottom nestled into his crotch.

He ignored the aching pain as blood pounded into his lap, grateful for the confining denim while waiting for her laboured breathing to even out—the renewed rush of heat not nearly as disturbing as the rush of tenderness.

Holding her wrist, he laid his arm across her body, careful not to touch any part of her that would make the torment worse. But the memory of spooning with her like this, after they'd made love that final time ten years ago, came flooding back to fill the void. Except that time his hands had caressed the compact bump of her belly, his head spinning with amazement and terror at what the future would hold.

Tortured thoughts of what she'd endured without him rose to the surface.

Eventually she stilled, the rigid line of her body softening against his.

Obviously, some remnant of the misguided kid he'd once been still remained. Because a part of him wanted to stay and hold her through the night, in case she had any more nightmares. But he couldn't go back and erase what he'd done, and she wouldn't want him here when she woke up in the morning.

So he'd just stay for a short while—until he was sure she was okay. Then he'd leave and get Mel to send over the divorce papers in the morning. So she'd lied about the miscarriage? Did he really want to know why? Delving into her reasons now wouldn't serve anyone's purpose.

But as he listened to the comforting murmur of her breathing his body relaxed against hers and all

his sound decisions drifted out into the night, shoot-
ing across the Hudson River, heading up towards the
Vineyard and back into fitful dreams.

CHAPTER TEN

SOMETHING HEAVY BECKONED Xanthe out of sleep. Deep, drugging, wonderful sleep that made her feel secure and happy.

Her eyelids fluttered open and her gaze focused on a hand. A large tanned hand with a tattoo of a ship's anchor on the thumb was holding hers down on the pillow, right in front of her face. The hand looked male. Very male. And very familiar.

She blinked, struggling to bring her mind into focus, and realised that a male arm, attached to the male hand, lay across her shoulders. She drew in a deep breath, the scent of clean sheets and clean man reminding her of the good dreams that had danced through her consciousness before waking. She shifted, aware of the long, muscular body wrapped around hers, and his deep breathing made the hair on the back of her neck prickle.

Dane.

Thin strands of sunlight shone through the slatted blinds, illuminating the hotel room's luxurious furnishings as the events of the evening before crowded in and her abdomen warmed, weighed down by the hot brick in her stomach.

She stole a moment to absorb the comfort of being cocooned in a man's arms for the first time in... She frowned. For the first time in a decade.

Dane had always gravitated towards her in his sleep. She'd always woken up in his arms during the brief weeks of their marriage. It was one of the things she'd missed the most. And this time she didn't have the stirrings of morning sickness to cut through her contentment.

She had a vague recollection of nightmares chasing her, and then his arms and his voice lulling her back to sleep.

Holding her breath, she shifted under his arm and inched her hand out from under the much larger one covering it.

The rumble of protest against her hair froze her in place.

Long fingers squeezed hers, before his thumb inched down her arm, sliding the sleeve of the T-shirt down to the elbow—the T-shirt that was supposed to be protecting her from the thoughts making her belly melt.

'You playing possum?' A gruff voice behind her head asked.

'I'm trying to.' She sighed, annoyed and at the same time stupidly aroused.

She could feel the solid bulge against her bottom, the unyielding wall of his chest that was sending delicious shivers of reaction up her spine.

'Mmm...' he mumbled, sounding half-asleep as his hand lifted and then settled on her thigh.

His calloused caress had goosebumps tingling to life as he trailed his hand under the hem of the T-shirt and rubbed across her hip.

Awareness settled between her legs and she rolled abruptly onto her back to halt his exploration.

His hand rested on her belly as he rose up on one elbow to peer down at her. His short hair was flattened on one side, and the stubble on his chin highlighted that perfect masculine dimple. Amusement and desire glinted in the impossible blue. Her breath squeezed under her diaphragm.

He'd always looked so gorgeous in the morning—all rumpled and sexy and usually a little surly. He'd never been much of a morning person, unlike her. But he didn't look surly now. He looked relaxed and devastatingly sexy.

'I didn't plan to stay the night,' he said, by way of explanation. 'But seeing as I'm here…'

His hand edged down, that marauding thumb brushing the top of her sex. Her belly trembled in anticipation.

'This isn't a good idea,' she murmured, trying to convince herself to push his hand away.

Pressing his face to her neck, he nuzzled kisses along her jaw. 'Nope.'

The tremor of awareness drew her the rest of the way out of sleep and into sharp, aching need. He cupped her, slid his fingers through her slick folds, locating the knot of desire with pinpoint accuracy.

She gasped and rolled towards him, letting him lift the soft cotton shirt over her head and throw it away.

He captured one aching nipple with his lips as his fingers continued to work their magic.

Memories assailed her of waking up just like this, with his hands and tongue and teeth beckoning her out of sleep and into ecstasy. She pushed back the rush of memory, the sapping tide of romanticism, until all that was left was the hot, hard demand of sexual need.

She desired Dane—she always had. But that was all it had ever been.

Reaching out, she cradled the bulge confined behind a layer of denim. 'Why are you wearing your jeans in bed?'

'Stop asking dumb questions,' he grumbled. 'And help me out of them.'

She didn't need any more encouragement. This was wrong, and they both knew it, but it didn't seem to matter any more. In a few short hours they will have declared the end of their marriage. And she wanted him here, now, more than she'd ever wanted any man. Just once more.

She released the button fly with difficulty, to find him long and hard beneath stretchy boxers.

'Take them off,' she demanded, pleased to hear the power, the assurance in her voice.

She was taking control. He couldn't walk all over her any more. And here was the proof.

But as he threw the covers back and divested himself of the last of his clothes she found herself feeling strangely vulnerable as he climbed over her, caging her in.

'Tell me exactly what you want, Red. I want to make you come so hard you scream.'

The words excited her beyond bearing. And terrified her, too. Reminding her of the boy who had once taken her to places no other man ever had.

She'd never been coy about sex, but she'd never been bold either—except with him.

Folding her hand around his huge length, she flicked her thumb across the tip, trying to regain control. Regain the power. Adrenaline rushed through her as his thick erection jerked against her palm.

His mouth took hers as his fingers delved into her hair and he angled her head to devour her. The scrape of his beard ignited tender skin…her tongue tangled with his.

He reached across her to grab a condom from the bedside table.

She took it from him. 'Let me.'

'Go ahead,' he said, relinquishing control.

The fire in his eyes was full of approval, and a desire that burned her to the core. No other man had ever desired her the way he had.

She fumbled with the foil packet, her skin flushing at his strained laugh.

He chuckled. 'You need more practice.'

She slipped the condom on, aware that she had never done this for another man. Determined not to let him know it. He wasn't special, He was just…filling a need. A need that she had neglected for far too long.

Her thoughts scattered, centring on his thumb as he began to stroke her again. Stroking her into a frenzy. One long finger entered her and she flinched slightly.

Evidence of their rough coupling the night before was still present, still there.

'Hey...' He cupped her cheek, forcing her to meet his eyes. 'Are you too sore for this?'

His concerned expression had her heartbeat kicking her ribs. Bringing with it a myriad of unwanted memories. His rough hand holding her hair, rubbing her back as she threw up in the motel toilet. Those lazy mornings when the nausea hadn't hit and he'd taken her slowly, patiently, watching her every response, gauging her every need and meeting it.

'I'm fine,' she said, precisely because she wasn't.

Don't be kind. Please don't be kind. I can't stand it.

'Uh-huh.' He didn't look convinced. Holding her, he rolled, flipping onto his back until she was poised above him, her knees on either side of his hips.

'How about *you* take charge this time?' he said, and she felt her heart expand in her chest.

But then his thumb located that pulsing nub and every thought flew out of her head bar none. *She had never been in charge of her hunger for him.*

He coaxed the orgasm forth as she sank down on his huge shaft.

'That's it, Red. Take every inch.'

He held her hips, lifting her as she parted round the thick length, almost unable to bear the feeling of fullness, of stretching, but unable to stop herself from sinking down again to take more, to take him right to the hilt.

His harsh grunts matched her moans as she rode him, increasing the tempo. A stunning orgasm was racing towards her. Her mind reeled as his gaze locked on hers, encouraging, demanding, forcing her over that perilous edge as he gave her one last perfect touch.

She sobbed, throwing her head back, her body shattering as she came hard and fast. She heard him shout out moments later, his penis pulsing out his release as his fingers dug into her thighs.

She fell on top of him, her forehead hitting his collarbone with a solid *thunk* as her heart squeezed tight.

She closed her eyes, her staggered breathing matching the pounding beat of her heart as his large hands settled on her back and stroked up to her nape. Blunt fingers massaged her scalp.

He laughed, the sound low and deep and self-satisfied. Warning bells went off, but they sounded faint and unimportant, drowned out by the glorious wave of afterglow.

'How about…before we finalise our divorce…' his deep voice rumbled against her ear '…we treat ourselves to a honeymoon?'

She lifted herself off him with an effort. 'What are you talking about?'

'I've got a week's vacation coming.' He brushed his fingers down her arms, setting off a trail of goose pimples and reigniting those damn birthday candles. 'I was supposed to be heading to Bermuda this afternoon, for a sailing trip to Nassau. I could postpone it for a couple of days.'

For a split second her endorphin-clouded mind actually considered it. Being with him—escaping from the endless stress and responsibilities of her job, from all the pain and regret of their past. But then her heart jumped in her chest and reality crashed in on her.

This was *Dane*. The man who had always been able to separate sex from intimacy in a way she never had. Or at least not with him.

She didn't hate him any more. And he still had the ability to seduce her and turn her into a puddle of lust with a single touch, a single look. She couldn't risk being alone with him for another hour, let alone for another night.

'I don't think so,' she said.

She climbed off him and bent to retrieve his discarded T-shirt, suddenly desperate for clothing. But his hand clamped on her wrist. His face was devoid of the lazy amusement of a moment ago.

'Why not?'

He looked genuinely irritated by her refusal, which told her all she needed to know.

'Because I have a company to run. I'm CEO of Carmichael's now—I can't afford to take time off,' she finished, giving him the face-saving answer.

She couldn't tell him the real reason—that she didn't want to risk spending time alone with him. He'd think she was nuts. Maybe she *was* nuts.

She was stronger, wiser and older now, with a healthy cynicism that should protect her from remaking the catastrophic mistakes of her youth. But the new knowledge that Dane had only abandoned her because he'd thought she'd abandoned *him* left a tiny sliver of opportunity for those old destructive feelings to take hold of her emotions again—especially coupled with more mind-altering sex.

She didn't want to be that idiot girl again, and if anyone could sway her back into the path of destruction it was a juggernaut like Dane. And the worst of it was *he* would remain unscathed. The way he always had before. For him, sex was always just sex—and that hadn't changed, or he would never have suggested another night of no-holds-barred sex after the tumult of the last twenty-four hours.

But why wouldn't he when *he* didn't have to worry about stirring up old feelings because he had never loved her the way she'd loved him? He'd only suggested marriage because of the guilt and responsibility he'd felt over her pregnancy—and, however her father had interfered in their break-up, it was obvious their marriage had been doomed to failure.

Deep down, she would always be a romantic—an easy target for a man like Dane who didn't have a single soft or sensitive or romantic bone in his body.

He'd never let her in. Had never let his guard down during the whole three months they'd lived in that motel.

He finally let go of her wrist and she scooted to the edge of the bed to put on the T-shirt, feeling awkward and insecure, reminded too much of that romantic child.

'So you're running daddy's company now?'

She dragged the T-shirt over her head. 'It's not his company any more. It's mine.'

Or it would be as soon as she had Dane's signature on those divorce documents and the controlling 6 per cent of the shares could be released to her.

She swallowed down a prickle of guilt at her deception. Dane had no claim on Carmichael's—it was simply a paperwork error. A paperwork error that, once corrected, he need never know about.

'He hated my guts when we were kids...'

The non sequitur sounded casual, but she could hear the bite in his voice and knew it was anything but.

What did he expect her to say? That her father had been a snob and had decreed Dane unsuitable? How could she defend Dane without compromising herself and her decision to take on Carmichael's after her father's death? The company had meant everything to her father and she understood that now—because it meant everything to *her*. And if a small voice in her head was trying to deny that and assert that there was more to life than running a successful business, it was merely an echo of that foolish girl who had believed that love was enough.

'He didn't hate you,' she said. 'I'm sure he just thought he was doing what was best for me.'

Even as she said the words they sounded hollow to her, but she refused to condemn her father. He had loved her in his own way—while Dane never had.

'Did it ever occur to you that if I'd been able to see you that day, things might have turned out differently?' He raised a knee and the casually draped sheet dipped to his waistline.

His expression was infuriatingly unreadable. As always.

'I don't see how.' She hesitated, trying to force thick

words out past the frog in her throat. 'And it worked out okay for both of us, so I have no regrets.'

She turned away from the bed, desperate not to be having this conversation. It would expose her. She didn't want him to know how hard it had been for her. How much losing him and their baby had hurt her at the time. And how much else it had eventually cost her.

But he reached over and snagged her wrist again. 'That's bullshit. And you want to know how I *know* it's bullshit?'

'Not particularly,' she said, far too aware of the way his thumb was stroking her pulse, hoping he couldn't feel it hammering in her wrist like the wings of a trapped hummingbird.

'Last night you had a nightmare about losing the baby,' he said. 'That's why I stayed. That's why I was here when you woke up. Maybe if I had been able to do that ten years ago, I wouldn't still need to do it now.'

Her pulse pummelled her eardrums. She wanted to ask him how he knew she'd been having a nightmare about the miscarriage. But she definitely didn't want to know how she'd given herself away in her sleep. She felt vulnerable enough already.

'You didn't need to stay. I would have been fine. I've had them before and…'

She realised her mistake when his expression hardened.

'How many times have you had them before?'

Too many.

'Not often,' she lied.

'That bastard.' His fury wasn't directed at her, but still she felt the force of his anger.

'It's okay. Really. I've come to terms with what happened.'

'Don't lie, Red.'

He hooked his thumb round her ear, brushing her hair back and framing her face. The gesture was gentle, and full of concern. Making her heart pulse painfully.

'You can lean on me—you know that, right?'

'I don't need to lean on you,' she said, denying the foolish urge to rest her head into the consoling palm and take the comfort he offered.

'What are you so scared of?' he said, cutting through the defences she'd spent ten years putting in place.

'I'm not scared.' How could he know that when he had never really known *her*? 'Why would I be?'

'I don't know—you tell me,' he said tightly. 'Why did you let me go on believing you had an abortion yesterday?'

She stiffened and pulled away from him. How could he still read her so easily?

'Why would I bother to correct you? I didn't think it mattered any more. It was so long ago.'

'Of course it matters. I deserve to know what really happened. Especially if you're still having nightmares because—'

'Why, Dane?' she interrupted. 'Why do you deserve to know? When you never wanted our baby the way I did?'

He tensed and something flashed over his face—something that might almost have been hurt. But it was gone so quickly she was sure she had misinterpreted it. Dane had never wanted the baby—that much she knew for sure.

'If you had, you would have demanded to see me,' she said, cutting off the painful thought. 'Instead of assuming I'd had an abortion.'

'I *did* demand to see you.' Temper flashed in his eyes. 'Your father had his goons throw me out.'

'He…*what?*' The breath left her lungs in a painful rush. Anguish squeezed her chest. 'Did they hurt you?'

She could still remember those men. They'd terrified her, even though her father had always insisted they were there to protect her.

His eyes narrowed, and the annoyed expression was one she recognised. If there was one thing Dane had always despised, it was anything remotely resembling pity.

'I handled myself,' he said.

She didn't believe him. At nineteen he'd been tough and muscular, and as tall as he was now, but he'd also been a lot skinnier, a lot less solid—still partly a boy for all his hard knocks. Four of those men against one of him would have done some serious damage.

She noticed the crescent-shaped scar cutting across his left eyebrow and knew it hadn't been there before— she'd once known every one of the scars on his body. The scars he would never talk about.

She pointed at the thin white mark bisecting his brow. 'Where did you get that scar?'

He shifted, avoiding her touch. She dropped her hand, aware of the heavy weight in her belly.

'I don't remember.'

He sounded unconcerned. But that guarded expression told a different story. He did remember—he just wasn't prepared to discuss it.

The hollow pain blossomed. Why was she pressing the point? Maybe because he'd held her last night, through her nightmare…making her feel weak and needy. And then made love to her this morning with such unerring skill, coaxing the exact response he'd wanted out of her.

He'd held all the power in their relationship and it was now brutally obvious he held it still.

'My father had no right to treat you that way,' she said. 'If you tell me what injuries you suffered I'll have my legal team work out suitable compensation.'

Paying him off suddenly seemed like the perfect solution. The only way to get herself free and clear of him and the emotions he stirred in her. Her only chance of acquiring the distance she'd surrendered so easily ever since walking into his office yesterday.

'Don't play the princess with me. I don't want your money. I never did. And I sure as hell don't need it any more.'

'It's a simple matter of compen—'

'You didn't do anything wrong,' he said, slicing through her objection. '*He* did. If anyone owes me an apology, it's him.'

'Well, he's been dead for five years. So you're not likely to get one.'

'I don't want an apology from a dead guy—what I want is for you to acknowledge what he did to us was wrong. Why is that so damn hard for you?'

She threw her hands up in the air. 'Fine. I agree what he did was wrong. Is that enough for you?'

'No. I want you to stay here with me.'

'What has that got to do with anything?'

'He split us up before we were ready. We've got a chance now to take some time to say goodbye to each other properly.'

His gaze flicked down her frame, and the inevitable flare of heat she felt in response made it doubly clear exactly what their goodbye was supposed to entail.

'We're both grown-ups now and we deserve to finish this thing right. Why can't you see that?'

Because I'm scared I might still care about you. Too much.

'I've told you—it's just bad timing.'

'Don't give me that. If you're running the company you can make time for this. But you won't. And I want to know why.'

'I won't because I don't *want* to spend time with you,' she shouted back, determined to mean it. 'If your ego can't accept that, that's your problem—not mine. We're over—we've been over for ten years.'

'Yet I can still make you come so hard you scream. And you haven't let another guy do that to you for five years. Five years is a heck of a long time.'

The blush flushed through her to the roots of her hair. His eyes went razor-sharp.

'What the…? Has it been *longer* than five years?'

How could he know that?

'I didn't say that.' She scrambled to deny it. Knowing she couldn't lie because he would read her like a book and know the truth instantly.

Dane had always been able to use her need for him against her. He'd never treated her like a wife when they were married. Had never been capable of opening up to her and sharing anything of himself with her. And she'd been so pathetically grateful for any sign that he cared about her at all, she'd found that romantic.

She knew the truth now, though—that his possessiveness, his protectiveness, hadn't been a sign of his love. It had simply been a sign of his need to claim ownership. If he ever found out that she'd never shared her bed with any other man but him, she'd be handing him a loaded gun.

'You don't have to say it,' he said. 'It's written all over your face.'

'Oh, shut up!' She stormed off, determined to lock herself in the bathroom before he discovered the humiliating truth and shot down the last remaining shreds of her composure.

His laugh followed her all the way into the shower cubicle.

Who knew Xanthe could be so cute when she was mad?

Dane let out a strained chuckle as she slammed the bathroom door behind her, then rubbed the heel of his palm over the ache in the centre of his chest. The choking feeling returned.

It shouldn't really matter to him that his wife hadn't slept with that many other guys, but somehow it did.

It also shouldn't matter to him that she didn't want to hang out at the hotel for another night.

He wasn't a possessive guy, or a particularly protective one. But with Xanthe it had always been different. Because he'd been her first. And she'd once been pregnant with his child.

And seeing her have that nightmare, knowing it wasn't the only one she'd had, had affected him somehow. Made him feel guilty for not being there when she'd needed him, even though his head was telling him it wasn't his fault.

She'd been stressed and exhausted when she'd arrived in his office yesterday. Enough to face-plant right in front of him. And in that moment she had reminded him of the girl she'd been—the girl he'd felt so in tune with because of the way she'd been bullied by her father. That girl had always been trying to please a guy who would never be pleased. And now it looked as if she was still doing it.

That had to be why she'd worked herself into the ground to take on her old man's company. She'd never had any interest in it back then. He didn't doubt she was good at her job—she'd always been smart and conscientious, and it seemed she'd added a new layer of ball-buster to the mix since then. But if she enjoyed it so much why didn't she have a life outside it?

He knew how easy it was to lose sight of your personal life, your personal well-being when you were building a business. He'd done the same in the last few years. Hell, he'd only managed a couple of short-term hook-ups since they'd split. But his company had been his dream right from when he was a little kid and he'd hung around down by the marina to avoid his father's belt.

And he was a lot tougher than Xanthe would ever be. Because he'd been born into a place where you hit the ground running or you just hit it—hard.

He knew how to take care of number one. He always had. Because no one else had wanted the job. Xanthe had always been way too open, way too eager to please. And it bugged him that she was still trying to please a dead man.

He didn't like seeing that hollow, haunted look lurking behind the tough girl facade. And she was still his wife until those papers were signed.

After getting dressed, he picked up his cell phone and keyed in his attorney's number. He'd promised to sign the damn papers, but who said he had to sign them straight away?

'Jack, hi,' he said, when his attorney answered on the second ring. 'About those papers I sent over yesterday…'

'I had a look at them last night,' Jack replied, cutting straight to the chase as usual. 'I was just about to call you about them.'

'Right. I've agreed to sign them, but I—'

'As your legal counsel, I'd have to advise against you doing that,' Jack interrupted him.

'Why?' he asked, his gut tensing the way it had when he was a kid and he'd been bracing himself for a blow from his old man's belt. 'They're just a formality, aren't they?'

'Exactly,' Jack replied. 'You guys haven't lived together for over ten years, and two to five years separation is the upper limit for most jurisdictions when it comes to contesting a divorce.'

'Then what's the deal with telling me not to sign the papers?'

Jack cleared his throat and shifted into lecture mode. 'Truth is, your wife doesn't require your signature on *anything* to get a divorce. She could have just filed these papers in London as soon as she found out about the failure to file the original documents and I would have gotten a heads-up from her legal representative. That's what got me digging a little deeper—I got to wondering why she'd come all the way to Manhattan to deliver them in person and that's when I found something curious buried in the small print.'

'What?' Dane asked, the hairs on his neck standing to attention.

The fact that Xanthe hadn't needed to bring the documents over in person had already occurred to him. That she hadn't needed to bring them at all seemed even more significant. But the anxiety jumping in his stomach wasn't making him feel good about that any more.

'There's a codicil stating that neither one of you will make a claim on any property acquired after the original papers should have been filed.'

'Then I guess I can quit worrying about her trying to claim back-alimony.' He huffed out a breath. He was not as pleased with the implication that Xanthe had made a point of not wanting any part of his success as he ought to be.

'Sure, but here's the thing—it goes on to state all the

assets that can't be claimed on. Why would she need to itemise those in writing? She'd have a hell of a legal battle trying to claim any of your property on the basis of a separation made years before your company even began trading. But that's when I got to thinking. What if it wasn't *your* property she was trying to protect but her own?'

'I don't get it. I couldn't make any claim on her property.'

Did she think he *wanted* her property? Her old man had once accused him of being a gold-digger. Of getting his daughter pregnant and marrying her to get his hands on Carmichael's money. Had she believed the old bastard? Was that why she'd let him go on believing she'd had an abortion? To punish him for something he hadn't done?

Anger and injured pride collided in his gut, but it did nothing to disguise the hurt.

'Turns out you're wrong about that,' Jack continued. 'You've got grounds to make a claim on her company. I just got off the phone with a colleague in the UK who checked out the terms of her father's will. A will that was written years before she even met you. One thing's for sure—it answers the question of why she came all the way over to Manhattan to get you to sign her divorce papers.'

As Dane listened to Jack lecturing him about the legalities and the terms of Charles Carmichael's will his stomach cramped and fury at the sickening injustice of it all started to choke him. The same futile fury he'd felt after the beating he'd taken all those years ago because he'd wanted to see his wife, to know what had happened to his child.

Each word Jack uttered felt like another blow he couldn't defend himself against. Suddenly he was furious with Xanthe as well as her old man. For making him feel like that again. Worthless and desperate, yearning for something he couldn't have.

She'd planned to play him all along by coming here. How much of what had happened in the last day had even been real? She'd said she didn't want to spend any more time with him. And now he knew why—because once those papers were signed she'd have the guarantee she needed that he couldn't touch her father's precious company.

She'd lied. Because she'd decided he didn't deserve the truth. She'd even accused him of not caring about their baby. And then…

He thought about her whimpers of need, those hot cries as she came apart in his arms. She hadn't just lied to him, she'd used his hunger for her against him. Turned him back into that feral kid begging for scraps from a woman who didn't want him. Then she'd slapped him down and offered to pay him off when he'd had the audacity to ask for one more night.

He signed off with Jack, then sat down and waited for her to come out of the bathroom. The bitterness of her betrayal tasted sour on his tongue.

The good news was he had more leverage now than he could ever have dreamt of. And he was damn well going to use it. To show her that *no one* kicked him around—not any more.

CHAPTER ELEVEN

IT TOOK XANTHE twenty minutes to realise she could not hide in the bathroom for the rest of her natural life.

She'd faced a hostile board for five years and her father's stern disapproval for a great deal longer. She could deal with one hot as hell boat designer.

But even so she jumped when a knock sounded on the door.

'You still in there or have you disappeared down the drain?'

The caustic tone was almost as galling as the flush that worked its way up her torso at the low rumble of his voice.

'I'll be out in a minute.'

'A package got delivered for you.'

Her clothes.

Hallelujah.

She reached for the bolt on the door, then paused.

'Could you leave it there?'

With the hotel's satin robe somewhere on the floor of the suite and his T-shirt neatly folded to give back to him on the vanity unit, all she had to cover her nakedness was a towel.

'Why don't you order us some breakfast?' she added, trying to sound unconcerned. Because clearly he was not going to do the decent thing and just leave her in peace.

'You want the package—you're gonna have to come out and get it.'

Blast the man.

Grasping the towel tight over her breasts, she flicked back the bolt and opened the door. She shoved the T-shirt at him, far too aware of his spectacular abs peeping out from behind his unbuttoned shirt.

He took it, but lifted the package out of reach when she tried to grab it. 'Not so fast.'

'Give me the package,' she demanded, using her best don't-mess-with-me voice—the one that had always worked so well in board meetings but seemed to be having no impact at all on the man in front of her. 'It has my clothes in it. If you still want to talk we can talk, but I refuse to discuss anything with you naked.'

Because look how well that had turned out the last time she'd done it.

He kept the package aloft. 'If I give you this, I want a promise that you'll come out of there.'

She frowned at him, noticing the bite in his tone. Something was off. Something was *way* off—the muscle in his jaw was working overtime to keep that impassive look on his face.

'What's wrong?'

'Not a thing,' he said, his jaw as hard as granite. 'Except that you've been sulking for a good half hour.'

She hadn't been sulking. She'd been considering her options—very carefully. But she was finished with

being a coward now. Better to face him and get whatever he had to discuss over with. Because standing in
a towel with that big male body inches away was not
helping.

She reached out for the package. 'Deal.'

He slapped it into her palm.

Whipping back into the bathroom, she locked the
door and leaned against it. Something was most definitely wrong. Where had the wry amusement gone?
That searing look he'd given her had been as hard as
it was hot.

Blowing out a breath, she got her new clothes out of
the packaging. Sitting in the bathroom wouldn't solve
anything. It was time to face the music and wrap this
up once and for all.

Five minutes later she walked back into the suite, feeling a lot more steady with the new jeans and T-shirt and
fresh underwear on. He'd donned his T-shirt and discarded the overshirt, but even covered, his pecs looked
impressive as they flexed against the soft cotton while
he levered himself off the couch.

She noticed the divorce papers on the coffee table in
front of him. He must have had them couriered over. Relief was mixed with a strange emptiness at the thought
that he'd already signed them. Which was, of course,
ridiculous.

'Sorry to keep you waiting,' she said, polite and distant, even though her body was already humming with
awareness. Clearly that would never change.

'Really?'

He still sounded surly. Maybe she should have come out a bit sooner.

She didn't dignify the question with an answer. Crossing the room to the coffee pot on the sideboard, she poured herself a cup to buy some time. Even after half an hour of prepping she didn't know what to say to him.

The tense silence stretched between them as she took a quick gulp of the hot liquid and winced. 'I see you still like your coffee strong enough to Tarmac a road,' she commented.

The unbidden memory made her fingers tremble. She turned to find him watching her.

'I don't know what you want from me, Dane. I've said I'm sorry for what my father did, for what happened. Obviously our break-up…' She paused, clarified. 'The way our break-up happened was regrettable. But I want to end this amicably. I can't stay in New York any longer.'

Because, however tempting it would be to indulge herself, let her body dictate her next move, she never wanted to be a slave to her libido again.

'That's why you came here? To end this amicably?'

It was a leading question. And, while it hadn't been the reason she'd boarded the plane yesterday morning at Heathrow, she felt an odd tightening in her chest at the thought of what they'd shared the day before and through the night. Stupid as it was, her heart skipped a beat.

Had she been kidding herself all along? Despite the implications for Carmichael's, she could have done this

whole process by proxy. It would have been simpler...
more efficient. But as soon as Bill had mentioned Dane's
name to her she'd been bound and determined to do it
in person. And she suspected her reasons were much
more complex than the ones she'd admitted to herself.

How much had her coming here *really* had to do with
the threat to Carmichael's? And how much to do with
that grief-stricken girl who had mourned the loss of
him as much as she had mourned the loss of their baby?

He had been the catalyst—the one who'd shown her
she was more, *could* be more than her father had ever
given her credit for. And, despite the shocks to her system in the last hours, she would always be grateful to
have discovered that he hadn't abandoned her the way
her father had wanted her to believe.

Placing the coffee mug back on the counter, she faced
him fully. 'Honestly? I think I needed to see you again.
And, as difficult as this has been—I'm sure for both of
us—I'm glad I did.'

'Yeah?'

'Yes.' Why did he still sound so annoyed?

'Nice speech. I guess that's my cue to sign these?'
He scooped the divorce papers up from the table. 'And
then get out of your way?'

'I suppose...' she said, feeling oddly ambivalent
about the papers, her pulse beginning to hammer at
her collarbone.

He didn't just sound surly now. He sounded furious. And he wasn't making much of an effort to hide it.

'Tough, because that's not gonna happen.' He ripped
the papers in two, then in two again, the tearing sound

echoing around the room. Then he flung the pieces at her feet.

'Why did you do that?' She bent to pick them up, her heart hammering so hard now she thought it might burst.

Grasping her arm, he hauled her upright. 'Because I'm not as dumb as you think I am. I know what your phoney divorce papers are really for. To stop me claiming the fifty-five per cent of your old man's company he left to *your husband* in his will.'

'But…' Her knees dissolved. The blow was made all the more devastating by the look of total disgust on his face.

'You didn't come here to end a damn thing *amicably*. You came here to play me.'

'That's not true.'

But even as she said it she could feel the guilt starting to strangle her. Because when she'd come here that was exactly what she'd intended to do.

'Well, it is partially true. But that was before I found out…'

'You think you can lie and cheat and say and do whatever the hell you want to get your way? Just like your old man? Well, you're gonna have to think again. Because *no one* screws with me any more.'

There were a million things she could say in her defence. A million things she wanted to say. But her throat closed, trapping the denial inside her. She felt herself shutting down in the face of his anger. Wanting to crawl away and make herself small and invisible. The way she had whenever her father had shouted at her, had bullied and belittled her, had derided her for being too soft, too sentimental, too much of a *girl*.

'I've got to hand it to you…the seduction was a nice touch.'

Heat seared her to the core as his gaze raked over her, as hot as it was derisive.

'You've certainly learned how to use that fit body to your advantage.'

The contemptuous comment felt like a smack in the face. Releasing the anger which had lain dormant for far too long.

'How dare you imply…?'

Hauling herself out of his arms, she slapped him hard across the face, determined to erase that smug smile.

His head snapped back on impact. And fire blazed in her palm.

But her anger faded as quickly as it had come, the volcanic lava turning to ash as he lifted a hand to his cheek to cover the red stain spreading across the tanned skin. His eyes sparked with contempt, and his powerful body rippled with barely controlled fury.

Shock reverberated through her.

He manipulated his jaw, then licked his lip, gathering the tiny spot of blood at the corner of his mouth. The nonchalant way in which he had accepted the blow made her feel nauseous. How many other times had he been hit before?

'So daddy's little princess finally learned how to fight back,' he said, the fury in his tone tempered by an odd note of regret.

The shock disappeared, to be replaced with weariness and a terrible yearning to turn back the clock. What were they doing to each other? She couldn't hate him any more—it hurt too much to go there again.

But how could he have such contempt for her? Know so little about who she'd been then and who she was now?

'Dane, I can explain. This isn't what it looks like.'

Except it was in some ways.

She reached for him, needing to soothe the blotchy mark she'd caused. He jerked away and brushed past her, heading for the door.

'It's *exactly* what it looks like.'

He opened the door, and part of her heart tore inside her chest. He was walking away from her again—the way he had once before. But she couldn't find the words to stop him, all her protests lodged inside her.

He paused at the door, fury still blazing in the ice-blue eyes. 'I never wanted your old man's money— or his crummy company. Which just makes it all the sweeter now that I can take a piece of it if I want to. Just for the hell of it. Don't contact me again.'

Xanthe collapsed onto the couch as the door slammed, her mind reeling and her whole body shaking.

She wrapped her arms around her midriff, taking in the unmade bed, the torn pieces of document on the carpet, the unfinished mug of black coffee. A gaping wound opened up in her stomach and threw her back in time to that dingy motel room in Boston. Lost and alone and terrified.

Tears squeezed past her eyelids as she sniffed back the choking sob that wanted to come out of her mouth.

If Dane followed through with his threat she might very well lose everything she'd worked so hard for in the last ten years. Even the *threat* of legal action would be enough to destroy her position as CEO. If the board ever found out she'd mismanaged this situation so catastrophically they would surely withdraw their support.

But far worse than the possibility of losing her job was that look of contempt as he'd accused her of being daddy's little princess.

Was that really what he'd thought of her all those years ago? That she was some spoilt little rich girl? Was that why he'd never trusted her with his secrets? Was that what he thought of her now, despite all she'd achieved?

And why did it sting so much to know he'd always thought so little of her?

She stood up and thrust shaky fingers through her hair, scrubbing away the tears on her cheeks.

No. Not again. She was not going to fold in on herself. Or let his low opinion of her matter.

Ten years ago stuff had happened that had been beyond their control. Her father's interference... The miscarriage... But there had been so much more they could have controlled but hadn't. And anyway the past was over now. Dane Redmond didn't mean anything to her any more.

Maybe she should have told him about the will as soon as she had discovered he hadn't abandoned her. She could see now that hadn't played well when he'd figured it out. But *he* was the one who had assumed she'd had an abortion, who had never trusted in her love, and *he* was the one who was threatening to take her company away from her. Why? Because she'd had the audacity to protect herself?

This was all about his bull-headed macho pride. Dane, in his own way, was as stubborn and unyielding as her father.

Well, she wasn't that timid, fragile, easily seduced child any more. And she was *not* going to sit around and let him crucify her and ruin everything she'd worked for.

She had the guts to stand up to him now. He was in for a shock if he thought this 'princess' wasn't tough enough to get him to sign the damn divorce papers and eliminate any threat to her company—even if she had to scour Manhattan to find him.

Four hours later, after a frantic trip to his offices and a fruitless interrogation of his tight-lipped PA, she discovered it wasn't going to be that easy.

Sitting in the first-class departure lounge at JFK, en route to St George, Bermuda, she felt a knot of anxiety start to strangle her as she contemplated how she was going to stay strong and resolute and indomitable if she was forced to confront her taciturn and intractable ex-husband on a yacht in the middle of the Atlantic...

CHAPTER TWELVE

'THERE, ON THE HORIZON—that has to be it.' Xanthe pointed at the yacht ahead of them and got a nod from the pilot boat operator she'd hired that afternoon at the Royal Naval Dockyard on Ireland Island, Bermuda. She pushed back the hair that had escaped her chignon and started to frizz in the island's heat.

The punch of adrenaline and purpose had dwindled considerably since her moment of truth at the hotel the day before—now the snarl of nerves was turning her stomach into a nest of vipers. The boat sped up, skipping over the swell. She held fast to the safety rail. The sea water sprinkling her face was nowhere near as refreshing as she needed it to be.

At least her madcap chase to find Dane and confront him was finally at an end, after a two-hour flight from JFK, a sleepless night at an airport hotel in St George, scouring the internet for possible places he might have harboured his boat, and then a three-hour taxi journey criss-crossing Bermuda as she checked out every possible option.

She'd arrived at the Royal Naval Dockyard on the

opposite tip of the island, the very last place on her list, at midday, with her panic starting to eat a hole in her stomach. The discovery that Dane had been there and just left had brought with it anxiety as well as relief at the thought of confronting him.

She gripped the rail until her knuckles whitened as the pilot boat pulled closer to the bobbing yacht.

At least her frantic transatlantic call to London at four that morning had confirmed Dane had yet to start any legal proceedings against her. So there was still time—if she could talk sense into him.

The gleam of steel stanchions and polished teak made the sleek vessel look magnificent as the blue-green of the water reflected off the fibreglass hull.

Her heart stuttered as she read the name painted in swirling letters on the side.

The Sea Witch.

The teasing nickname whispered across her consciousness.

'I'm under a spell...you've bewitched me, Red... you're like a damn sea witch.'

The muscles of her abdomen knotted as she tried to erase the memory of his finger circling her navel as he'd smiled one of his rare smiles while they'd lain on the beach at Vineyard Sound together, a lifetime ago, and he'd murmured the most—and probably the only— romantic thing he'd ever said to her.

Beads of sweat popped out on her upper lip as she spotted Dane near the bow, busy readying the boat's rigging. She'd caught him just in time. His head jerked round as the pilot boat's rubber bumpers butted the yacht's hull and the boat's captain shouted to announce their arrival.

She shook off the foolish memories and slung her briefcase over her shoulder. She had a short window of opportunity. She needed to get on board before Dane could object or the pilot boat's captain would realise the story she'd spun him about being a guest who had missed the sailing was complete fiction.

Grabbing hold of the yacht's safety line, she clambered into the cockpit. She quickly unclasped her life jacket and flung it back to the pilot boat.

'I can take it from here—thank you so much!' she shouted down to the captain.

The man glanced at Dane, who had finished with the rigging and was bearing down on her from the other end of the boat. 'You sure, ma'am?'

Not at all.

'Positive,' she said, flinching when Dane's voice boomed behind her.

'What the *hell* are you doing here?'

She ignored the shout and kept her attention on the pilot boat's captain. 'I'll be in touch in approximately twenty minutes. And I'll double your fee if you leave us now.'

Dane didn't want her on board, which meant he would have to listen to reason. It wasn't much of a bargaining chip, but it was the only one she had.

'Okay, ma'am.' The pilot boat captain tipped his hat as his nervous gaze flicked to Dane and back. 'If you say so.'

The boat's engine roared to life. The captain had

peeled the nimble vessel away from the yacht, obviously keen to avoid unnecessary confrontation, and was headed towards the marina when Dane reached her.

'Where is he going?'

She turned to face him. 'He's returning to the harbour and will come to pick me up once I give him the signal.'

Her rioting heartbeat slammed into her throat.

He looked furious, his face rigid with temper.

'Is this some kind of joke? Get off my boat.'

'No.' She locked her knees, forcing her chin up. 'Not until you sign the divorce papers.' She dumped the briefcase at his feet. 'I have a new set in there to replace the ones which fell victim to your temper tantrum at the hotel.'

His scowl darkened at the patronising comment, and the punch of adrenaline she'd felt after he'd stormed out on her returned full force. Bolstering her courage.

That's right, you don't have the tiniest notion who you're dealing with now.

The slap of the sea against the hull and the cry of a nearby seabird pierced the silence as the seconds ticked by—seeming to morph into hours—and the rigid fury rippling through him threatened to ignite. With his tall, muscular body towering over her, and the dark stubble covering his rigid jaw he looked more disreputable than a pirate and a lot more volatile.

She forced herself to resist flinching under the contemptuous appraisal as his gaze scoured her skin. Okay, maybe she'd underestimated the extent of his anger. But showing him any weakness would be the height of folly, because Dane would exploit it. The way he had exploited it once before. When she'd been young and naive and completely besotted with him.

His T-shirt was moulded to the wall of pecs in the breeze, the pushed-up sleeves revealing his tattoo, which bulged as he crossed his arms over his broad chest and stared her down. The sweet spot between Xanthe's thighs hummed, the unwanted arousal tangling with the punch of adrenaline to make anxiety scream under her breastbone like a crouching tiger waiting to pounce.

'What makes you think I won't haul you overboard?'

The ice-blue of his eyes made her brutally aware that this was no idle threat.

'Go ahead and try it.' She braced herself, prepared for the worse, bunching her hands into fists by her side. After the last twenty-four hours spent chasing him across the Atlantic she wasn't going to give up without a fight.

And, if the worst came to the worst, she could survive the two-mile swim back to the marina...

If she absolutely had to.

What the ever-loving—?

Dane cut off the profanity in his head, desire already pooling in his groin like liquid nitrogen.

To say he was shocked to see Xanthe was an understatement of epic proportions. Maybe not as stunned as when she'd shown up in Manhattan to inform him they were still married. But close.

She was the only woman, apart from his mother,

who had ever managed to hurt him. And while he knew she couldn't hurt him any more, because he was wise to her, he hadn't planned to test the theory. Especially on the vacation he had been looking forward to for months. Hell, *years*.

This was supposed to be a chance for him to get some much needed R & R. To enjoy the simplicity of being out on the water with nothing to worry about but keeping his course steady and the wind in his sails.

But as she stood in front of him, her lush hair dancing around her head in a mass of fire and those feline eyes glittering with defiance, he couldn't deny the leap of adrenaline.

When was the last time a woman had challenged him or excited him this much? Xanthe was the only one who had ever come close. But the girl he'd married was a shadow of the woman she was now.

They'd always been sexually compatible. But that firecracker temper of hers was something he'd only ever seen small glimpses of ten years ago—on those rare occasions when she'd stood up to him.

Unfolding his arms, he cracked the rigid line of his shoulders in a shrug and headed back towards the bow.

Big deal—she had more guts than he'd expected. He'd see how far that got her once she discovered he wasn't going to play ball.

Ducking under the mainsail, he set about untying the line he'd secured to the anchor chain and then pressed the button to activate the yacht's windlass.

'What are you doing?'

The high-pitched squeak of distress from over his shoulder told him she'd followed him.

'Weighing anchor,' he said, stating the obvious as he lifted the anchor the rest of the way into the boat, then marched back past her. 'You've got two minutes to call your guy before we head for open water.'

She scrambled after him. 'I'm not getting off this boat until you agree to sign those papers.'

He swung round and she bumped into his chest. She stumbled back to land on the bench seat of the cockpit, her cheeks flushed with a captivating mix of shock and awareness.

Arousal powered through his system on the heels of adrenaline.

'I'm not signing a damn thing.'

Taking the wheel, he adjusted the position of the boat until the breeze began to fill the mainsail.

'It's a four-day trip to the Bahamas, which is where I'm headed. With nowhere to stop en route. You want to be stuck on a boat with me for four days, that's up to you. Either that or you can swim back to the marina.'

He cast a look over his shoulder, as if assessing the distance.

'You're a strong swimmer. You should be able to make it by sunset.'

The mulish expression on her face was so priceless he almost laughed—until he remembered why she was there. To protect the company of a man who had treated him like dirt.

She glared back at him. 'I'm not budging until you sign those papers. If you think I'm scared of spending four days on a yacht with you, you're very much mistaken.'

The renewed pulse of reaction in his crotch at this ball-busting comment forced him to admire her fighting spirit. And admit that the fierce temper suited her.

Unfortunately for her, though, she'd chosen the wrong balls to bust.

The mainsail stretched tight and the boat lurched forward.

She gripped the rail, and the flash of panic that crossed her face was some compensation for the fiery heat tying his guts in knots as the yacht picked up speed.

'Yeah, well, maybe you should be,' he said, realising he wasn't nearly as mad about the prospect as he had been when she'd climbed aboard the yacht.

She'd chosen to gatecrash his solo sailing holiday and put them both into a pressure cooker situation that might very quickly get out of control. But if it did, why the hell should *he* care?

Doing the wild thing with Xanthe had never been a hardship. And seeing the unwanted arousal in her eyes now had taken some of his madness away, because it proved one incontrovertible fact. What had happened between them in that hotel room had been as spontaneous and unstoppable for her as it had been for him.

He wasn't going to sign her phoney papers because that would be the same as admitting she'd been right not to trust him with the truth back in Manhattan. That her father had been right not to trust him all those years ago, too.

Charles Carmichael had accused him of being a gold-digger, of being after the Carmichael money, and his daughter must believe it too or she wouldn't have tried to trick him into signing those papers.

He was a rich man now—he could probably buy and sell her precious Carmichael's twenty times over—but even as a wild-eyed kid, starved of so many things, he'd never asked for a cent from her *or* her old man.

Xanthe had been his once—she'd insisted she loved him. But even so a part of her had stayed loyal to her old man or she would have asked questions when her father had told her lies about him. She would have tried to contact him after the miscarriage. She wouldn't have let him go on believing she'd had an abortion up to two days ago. And she sure as hell wouldn't need any guarantee that he wasn't going to rip her off for 55 per cent of a company he had never wanted any part of.

If she wanted to spend the next four days pretending she was immune to him, immune to the attraction between them, so be it.

They'd see who broke first.

Because it sure as hell wasn't going to be him.

Exhaustion and nerves clogged Xanthe's throat as the boat bounced over the swell. She bit down on her anxiety as she watched the land retreat into the distance. She'd come all this way to reason with him—and argue some sense into him. And she'd do it. Even if she had to smack him over the head with a stanchion.

'I apologise for not telling you about my father's will.' She ground out the words, which tasted bitter on her tongue. Her ability to sound contrite and subservient, which was probably what he expected, had been lost somewhere over the Atlantic Ocean. 'I should have been straight with you once I knew you hadn't abandoned me ten years ago, the way my father led me to believe.'

He'd put his sunglasses on, and his face was an impassive mask as he concentrated on steering the boat—making it impossible for her to tell if her speech was having any impact.

The strong, silent treatment, which she had been treated to so many times in the past, only infuriated her more, while also making greasy slugs of self-doubt glide over her stomach lining.

She breathed deeply, filling her lungs with the sea air. Stupid how she'd never realised until now how easily he had undermined her confidence by simply refusing to communicate.

She dug her teeth into her bottom lip.

Not any more.

She wasn't that giddy girl, desperate for any sign of affection. And she wasn't getting off his precious boat until she had what she'd come for: namely, his signature on the replacement documents she had stuffed in her briefcase so she could end their marriage and any threat of legal action.

She glanced past him, back towards the mainland. Her pulse skipped a beat as she realised the pilot boat had disappeared from view and that Ireland Island was nothing more than a haze on the horizon dotted by the occasional giant cruise ship.

She pulled in a staggered breath, let it out slowly. The plan had been to get Dane's signature on the divorce documents—not to end up getting stuck on a yacht with him for four days.

She'd expected him to be uncooperative. What she *hadn't* expected was for him to call her bluff. Somewhere in the back of her mind she'd convinced herself that once she got in his face he'd be only too willing to end this charade.

But as the spark of sexual awareness arched between them, and the hotspot between her thighs began to throb in earnest, she realised she'd chronically underestimated exactly how much of an arrogant ass he could be.

The one thing she absolutely could *not* do was let him know how much erotic power he still wielded.

'You don't want me here, and I don't want to be here. So why don't we just end this farce and then we never have to see each other again?'

His gaze finally lowered to hers. The dark lenses of his sunglasses revealed nothing, but at least he seemed to be paying her some attention at last.

Progress. Or so she thought until he spoke.

'I don't take orders, Princess.'

The searing look was meant to be insulting, with the cruel nickname adding to her distress. Her anxiety spiked.

'Fine. You refuse to meet me even halfway...' She scooped the briefcase off the bench seat in the cockpit. 'I guess you're stuck with me.'

She headed below decks.

It wasn't a retreat, she told herself staunchly, simply a chance to refuel and regroup.

The cool air in the cabin's main living space felt glorious on her heated skin as she took a moment to catch her breath and calm her accelerated heartbeat.

But her belly dropped to her toes and then cinched into tight, greasy knots as her eyes adjusted to the low lighting and she took in the space they would be sharing for the next four days.

The yacht had looked huge from the outside, but Dane had obviously designed it with speed in mind. While the salon was luxuriously furnished in the best fabrics and fittings, and boasted a couch, a table, shelves crammed with books and maps, a chart table and a well-appointed galley equipped with state-of-the-art appliances, it was a great deal snugger than she had anticipated.

The man was six foot three, with shoulders a mile wide, for goodness' sake. How on earth was she going to fit in a space this compact with him without bumping up against that rock solid body every time the boat hit a wave?

And then she noticed the door at the end of the space, open a crack onto the owner's cabin, where a huge mahogany carved bed took up most of the available space, its royal blue coverlet tucked into the frame with military precision.

A hot brick of panic swelled in her throat, not to mention other more sensitive parts of her anatomy. She swallowed it down.

Dane wouldn't be spending much time below decks, she reasoned. No solo sailor could afford to spend more than twenty minutes at a time away from the helm if they were going to keep a lookout for approaching vessels or other maritime dangers. And she had no plans to offer to share the load with him, given she was effectively here against her will—not to mention her better judgement.

Dumping her briefcase, she crossed into the galley and flung open the fridge to find it stocked—probably by his staff—with everything she could possibly need to have a five-star yachting vacation at his expense.

He'd accused her of being a princess, so it would serve him right if she played the role to the hilt.

It didn't matter if the living space was compact. It had all the creature comforts she needed to while away her hours on board in style until he saw reason. With Dane occupied on deck, she could use this as her sanctuary.

After finding a beautifully appointed spare berth, with its own bathroom, she cleaned up and stowed her briefcase. Returning to the galley, she cracked open one of the bottles of champagne she'd found in the fridge, poured herself a generous glass and made herself a meal fit for a queen—or even a princess—from the array of cordon bleu food.

But as she picked at her meal her heartbeat refused to level off completely.

How exactly was she going to dictate terms to a man who had always refused to follow any rules but his own? A man she couldn't get within ten feet of without feeling as if she were about to explode?

Dane held fast to the wheel and scanned the water, blissfully empty and free of traffic now they'd left Ireland

Island and the pocket cruisers and day trippers behind.
He wheeled to starboard. The sail slapped against the
mast, then drew tight as the boat harnessed the wind's
power. He tipped his head back as *The Sea Witch* gathered speed. Elation swelled as the dying sun burned his
face and the salt spray peppered his skin.

Next stop the Bahamas.

What had he been thinking, waiting so long to get
back on the water?

But then his gaze dropped to the door to the cabin,
which had been firmly shut ever since Xanthe had
stormed off a couple of hours ago.

He imagined her sulking down there, and wondered
if she planned to hide away for the rest of the trip.

The boat punched a wave and the jolt shimmered
through his bones.

His heartbeat sped up. Her little disappearing act
confirmed what he already knew—that he wasn't the
only one who'd felt the snap and crackle of that insane
sexual chemistry sparking between them when she'd
arrived. The fact he was the only one prepared to admit
it gave him the upper hand.

He sliced the boat across the swell and felt the hull
lurch into the air.

She'd made a major miscalculation if she thought
they would be able to avoid it on a fifty-five-foot boat,
even if she planned to hide below decks for the duration.

Switching on the autopilot as the sun finally disappeared below the horizon, he ventured below—to find
the salon empty and the door to the spare berth firmly
shut. But he could detect that subtle scent of spring

flowers that had enveloped him two nights ago, when he'd been wrapped around her in sleep.

He rubbed his chin, feeling two days' worth of scruff. He imagined her fingernails scraping over his jaw. What was that saying about opposites attracting?

They were certainly opposites—him a 'wharf rat' who had made good and her the princess ballsy enough to run a multinational company, even if she *was* only doing it to please her old man. But the attraction was still there, and stronger than ever.

He wasn't going to push anything because he didn't have to. She would come to him—the way she had before. And then they'd see exactly who needed who.

He grabbed a beer from the fridge, a blanket from his cabin and the alarm clock he kept on hand to wake him up during the night while he was on watch. But as he headed back up on deck, ready to bed down in the cockpit, he spotted an artfully arranged plate of fancy deli items sitting on the galley counter covered in sandwich wrap. Next to it was an open bottle of fizz, with a note attached to it.

For Dane, from his EX-wife.
Don't worry, the princess hasn't poisoned it…yet!

He coughed out a gruff chuckle. 'You little witch.'

But then the memory of the meals she'd always had waiting for him in their motel room when he'd got back from another day of searching for work slammed into him. And the rueful smile on his lips died. Suddenly all he could see was those brilliant blue-green eyes of hers, bright with excitement about the pregnancy. All he could hear was her lively chatter flowing over him as he watched her hands stroke the smooth bump of her stomach and shovelled up the food she'd made for him in silence. Too scared to tell her the truth.

Heat flared in his groin, contradicting the guilt twisting in his gut as the crushing feeling of inadequacy pressed down on him.

That agonising fear felt real again—the fear of going another day without finding a job, the terror that had consumed him at the thought that he couldn't pay their motel bill, let alone meet the cost of Xanthe's medical care when the baby arrived.

Putting the beer back in the fridge, he chugged down a gulp of the expensive champagne and let the fruity bubbles dissolve the ball of remembered agony lodged in his throat.

Get a grip, Redmond.

That boy was long gone. He didn't have anything to prove any more. Not to Xanthe, not to himself, not to anyone. He'd made a staggering success of his life. Had worked like a dog to get to college and ace his qualification as a maritime architect, then developed an award-winning patent that with a clever investment strategy had turned a viable business into a multimillion-dollar marine empire—not to mention acing the America's Cup twice with his designs.

He had more than enough money now to waste on bottles of pricey fizz that he rarely drank. Getting hung up on the past now was redundant.

She'd thought she loved him once and, like the sad

little bastard he'd been then, he'd sucked up every ounce of her affection—all those tender touches, the adoring looks, all her sweet, stupid talk about love and feelings.

But he wasn't that sad little bastard any more. He knew exactly what he wanted and needed now. And love didn't even hit the top ten.

He sat on deck, wolfing down the food she'd made for him and watching the phosphorescent glow of the algae shine off the water in the boat's wake while a very different kind of hunger gnawed at his gut.

He didn't need Xanthe's love any more, but her body was another matter—because, whether she liked it or not, they both knew that had always and *would* always belong to him.

CHAPTER THIRTEEN

XANTHE STEADIED HERSELF by slapping a hand on the table the following morning and glared at the hatch as the boat's hull rocked to one side. How fast was he driving this thing? It felt as if they were flying.

Luckily she'd already found her sea legs which, to her surprise and no small amount of dismay, were just where she'd left them the last time she'd been sailing— ten years ago. With Dane.

The boat lurched again, but her stomach stayed firmly in place.

Don't get mad. That had been her mistake yesterday. She needed to save herself for the big battles—like getting him to sign the divorce papers. Provoking him was counterproductive.

After a night of interrupted sleep, her body humming with awareness while she listened to him moving about in the salon on his short trips below deck, she knew just how counterproductive.

Given the meteoric rise in the temperature during their argument yesterday, she needed to be careful. Knowing Dane, and his pragmatic attitude to sex, he wouldn't exert too much effort to keep the temperature down, even if it threatened to blaze out of control. So it would be up to her to do that for both of them.

Xanthe poured herself a mug of the strong coffee she'd found brewing on the stove and added cream and sugar, adjusting to the sway of the boat like a pro.

While she wasn't keen to see Dane, she couldn't stay down here indefinitely. Early-morning sunlight glowed through the windows that ran down the side of the boat. Each time the hull heeled to starboard she could see the horizon stretching out before them.

Her pulse jumped and skittered, reminding her of the days they'd spent on the water before, and how much she'd enjoyed that sense of freedom and exhilaration. Of course back then she'd believed Dane would keep her safe. That he cared about her even if he couldn't articulate it.

She knew better now.

Good thing she didn't need a man to keep her safe any longer.

She dumped the last of the coffee into the sink and tied her hair back in a knot.

She wasn't scared of Dane, or her reaction to him, so it was way past time she stopped hiding below deck.

Even so, her heart gave a definite lurch—to match the heel of the boat—when she climbed out of the cabin and spotted Dane standing at the wheel. On the water, with his long legs braced against the swell, his big capable hands steering the boat with relaxed confidence and his gaze focused on the horizon, he looked even more dominant and, yes—damn it—sexy. Her pulse jumped, then sank into her abdomen, heading back to exactly where she did not need it to be.

She shut the door to the cabin with a frustrated snap. His gaze dropped to hers. Her face heated at the thorough inspection.

'You finished sulking yet, Princess?' His deep voice carried over the flap of canvas and the rush of wind.

Her temper spiked at the sardonic tone. 'I wasn't sulking,' she said. 'I was having some coffee and now I plan to do some sunbathing.'

After a night lying awake in her cabin and listening to him crewing the boat alone, she had planned to offer to help out this morning. She needed to get him to sign those papers, and she'd never been averse to good honest work, but his surly attitude and that 'princess' comment had fired up her indignation again.

She'd be damned if she'd let his snarky comments and his low opinion of her and her motives get to her.

Ignoring him, she faced into the wind, letting it whip at her hair and sting her cheeks. The sea was empty as far as the eye could see, the bright, cloudless blue of the sky reflecting off the brilliant turquoise water. She licked her lips, tasted salt and sun…and contemplated making herself a mimosa later.

Gosh, she'd missed this. Despite having the fellow traveller from hell on board, maybe this trip wouldn't be a complete nightmare. But as she reached to swing herself up onto the main deck, a bulky life jacket smacked onto the floor of the cockpit in front of her.

'No sunbathing, princess, until you put that on and clip yourself to the safety line.'

She swung round. 'I'm not going to fall off. I'm not an amateur.'

'How long since you've been on a boat?'

'Not that long,' she lied.

She didn't want him to know she hadn't been sailing since they'd parted. He might think her enforced abstinence had something to do with him.

'Uh-huh? How long is "not that long"? Less than ten years?'

She sent him her best death stare. But the hotspots on her cheeks were a dead giveaway.

'Yeah, I thought so,' he said, doing his infuriating mind reading thing again. 'Now, put on the PFD or get below.'

'No. There's barely a ripple on the water. I don't need to wear one.' He was just doing this out of some warped desire to show her who was boss. 'If it gets at all choppy I'll put it on straight away,' she added. 'I'm not an idiot. I have no desire to end up floating around in the middle of the Atlantic.'

Especially as she wasn't convinced he'd bother to pick her up. But she refused to be bullied into doing something completely unnecessary just so *he* could feel superior.

Instead of answering her, he clicked a few switches on the wheel's autopilot and headed towards her.

She pressed against the hatch to avoid coming into contact with that immovable chest again as he reached past her for the jacket. She got a lungful of his scent. The clean smell was now tinged with the fresh hint of sea air.

Hooking the jacket with his index finger, he dangled it in front of her face.

'Put it on. Now.'

Her jaw tightened. 'No, I will not. *You're* not wearing one.'

'This isn't a negotiation. Do as you're told.'

Temper swept through her at his dictatorial tone.

'Stop behaving like a caveman.' She planted her feet, all her good intentions to rise above his goading flying off into the wild blue Caribbean yonder.

Once upon a time she would have been only too willing to do anything he said, because his certainty, his dominance had been so seductive. Not any more.

The backs of her knees bumped against the seat of the cockpit as he loomed over her. Traitorous heat blossomed between her legs as she got another lungful of his exquisite scent. Fresh and salty and far too enticing.

'The hard way it is, then,' he announced, flinging the jacket down.

Realising his intention, she tried to dodge round him—but he simply ducked down and hiked her over his shoulder.

She yelped. Dangling upside down, eyeballing tight male buns in form-fitting shorts, as she rode his shoulder blade.

Finally getting over her shock enough to fight back, she punched his broad back with her fists as he ducked under the boom and hefted her towards the hatch.

'Put me down this instant!'

He banded an arm across her legs to stop her kicking. 'Keep it up, princess, and I'm tossing you overboard.'

She stopped struggling, not entirely sure he wouldn't carry out his threat, and deeply disturbed by the shocking reaction to his easy strength and the delicious scent of soap and man and sea.

Damn him and his intoxicating pheromones.

He swung her round to take the steps. 'Mind your head.'

When he finally dumped her in the salon she scrambled back, her cheeks aflame with outrage.

The tight smile did nothing to disguise the muscle jumping in his jaw and the flush of colour hitting tanned cheeks. She wasn't the only one far too affected by their wrestling match.

'Are you completely finished treating me like a two-year-old?'

She absorbed the spike of adrenaline when his nostrils flared.

'You don't want to be treated like a toddler?' His voice rose to match hers. 'Then don't act like one. You want to go on deck, you wear the jacket.'

'Being stronger and bigger than me does *not* make you right,' she said, her voice gratifyingly steely...or steely enough, despite the riot of sensations running through her. 'Until you give me a valid reason I'm not wearing it. You'll just have to keep carrying me down here.' Even if having his hands on her again was going to increase the torment. 'Let's see how long it takes for that to get *really* old.'

She stood her ground, refusing to be cowed. This stand-off was symptomatic of everything that had been wrong with their relationship the first time around.

She'd given in too easily to every demand, had never stuck up for herself. Never made him explain himself about anything—which was exactly how they'd ended up being so easily separated by her father's lies and half-truths.

Dane had threatened her company and refused to listen to reason, all to teach her a lesson about honesty and integrity—well, she had a few lessons to teach *him*. About respect and self-determination and the fine art of communication.

She wasn't a doormat any more. She was his equal.

'If you want me to wear it, you're going to have to explain to me why I need to when you don't. And then *I'll* decide if I'm going to put it on.'

He cursed under his breath and ran his hand over his hair, frustration emanating from him.

Just as she was about to congratulate herself for calling him on his Neanderthal behaviour, he replied.

'We're sailing against the prevailing winds, which means the swell can be unpredictable. I know when to brace because I can see what's coming. Without a jacket on you could go under before I could get to you.'

'But…that's…' She opened her mouth, then closed it again. 'Why didn't you just say that to start with?' she finally managed, past the obstruction in her throat.

He looked away, that muscle still working overtime in his jaw.

And the melting sensation in her chest, the sharp stab of vulnerability, gave way to temper and dismay. Why had it always been so hard for him to give her even the smallest sign that he cared? It was a question that had haunted her throughout their relationship ten years ago. It was upsetting to realise it haunted her still.

'You know why.'

His eyes met hers, the hot gaze dipping to brand the glimpse of cleavage above the scooped neck of her T-shirt. Heat rushed through her torso, darting down to make her sex ache.

He cupped her cheek, his thumb skimming over her bottom lip, the light in his eyes now feral and hungry. 'Because when I'm with you not a lot of thinking goes on.'

'Don't…' She jerked away from his touch, desperate to dispel the sensual fog. But it was too late. His compelling scent was engulfing her, saturating her senses and sending pheromones firing through her bloodstream.

Her breathing became ragged, her chest painfully tight, as arousal surged through her system.

'Quit pretending you don't want it, too,' he said as he watched her, the lust-blown pupils darkening the bright blue of his irises to black.

'I…I don't.' She cleared her throat, disgusted when her voice broke on the lie. 'We're not doing this again. That's not why I'm here.'

If they made love she was scared it would mean more than it should. To her, at least. And she couldn't risk that.

'Then stay out of my way,' he said. 'Or I'm going to test that theory.'

He walked away, heading back on deck.

'I'm not staying below decks for three days!' she

shouted after him, gathering the courage that had been in such short supply ten years ago.

So what if she still wanted him? She couldn't let him control the terms of this negotiation. If she didn't speak out now she'd be no better than the girl she'd been then, ready to accept the meagre scraps he'd been willing to throw her way.

'I came here to save my company,' she added as he mounted the steps, still ignoring her. 'If you think I'm going to sit meekly by while you attempt to steal fifty-five per cent of it, you can forget it.'

His head jerked round, the scowl on his face going from annoyed to furious in a heartbeat, but underneath it she could see the shadow of hurt.

'I didn't want a cent from your old man when I was dead broke. Why the hell would I want a part of his company *now*?' he said as he headed back towards her.

She'd struck a nerve—a nerve she hadn't even realised was still there.

'Then why did you threaten to sue for a share of it?' she fired back, determined not to care about his hurt pride.

She had nothing to feel ashamed of. *She* wasn't the one who had stormed out of their hotel room claiming he was going to sue her just for the hell of it.

'I never said I was going to sue for anything,' he added. 'You made that assumption all on your own.'

'You mean...' Her mouth dropped open. Was he saying she'd come all this way and got stuck on a yacht with him for no reason? 'You mean you're *not* planning to take legal action?'

'What do you think?'

The concession should have been a relief, but it wasn't, the prickle of shame becoming a definite yank. She'd always known how touchy he was about her father's money, but how could she have forgotten exactly how important it had always been to him never to take anything he hadn't earned?

'Then why wouldn't you sign the divorce papers?' she asked, trying to stay focused and absolve her guilt.

How could she have known that his insecurities about money ran so deep when he'd never once confided in her about where they came from? If he'd simply signed the papers in Manhattan, instead of going ballistic, she never would have made the assumption that he intended to sue for the shares in the first place.

'And why won't you sign them now?'

'Your *phoney* divorce papers, you mean?'

'They're not phoney. They're just a guarantee that—'

'Forget it.'

He cut off her explanation, the scowl on his face disappearing to be replaced with something else—something that made no sense. He didn't care about her, he never really had, so what was there to regret?

'I'm not signing any papers that state I can't claim those shares if I want to.'

'But that's just being contrary. Why wouldn't you sign them if you don't want the shares?' she blurted out.

'I don't know,' he said, his tone mocking and thick with resentment. 'Why don't you try figuring it out?'

She didn't have to figure it out, though. Because it suddenly all became painfully obvious.

He expected her to *trust* him. In a way he'd never trusted her.

The searing irony made her want to shout her frustration at him, but she bit her lip to stop the brutal accusation coming out of her mouth.

Because it would make her sound pathetic. And it might lead to her having to ask herself again the heartbreaking question that had once nearly destroyed her.

Why had he never been able to believe her when she'd told him she loved him?

She refused to butt her head against that brick wall again—the brick wall he had always kept around his emotions—especially as it was far too late to matter now.

But then he touched her hair, letting a single tendril curl round his forefinger. The gentleness of the gesture made her heart contract in her chest, and the combination of pain and longing horrified her.

He gave a tug, making the punch of her pulse accelerate. And the yearning to have his mouth on hers became almost more than she could bear.

'Dane, stop,' she said, but the demand sounded like a plea.

She placed her palms on his waist, brutally torn as she absorbed the ripple of sensation when his abdominal muscles tensed under her hands.

'Don't push me, Red,' he murmured, his lips so close she could almost taste them. 'Or I'm gonna make you prove exactly how much you don't want me.'

For tantalising seconds she stood with desire and longing threatening to tear her apart. She should push him away. Why couldn't she?

But then he took the choice away from her.

Cursing softly, he let her go.

She watched him leave, feeling dazed and shaky. She'd fallen under Dane's sensual spell once before and it had come close to destroying her…because he'd always refused to let her in.

But until this moment she'd had no idea exactly how much danger she was in of falling under it again. Or that all those tangled needs and desires to understand him, to know the reasons why he couldn't love her or trust her, had never truly died.

Dane yanked the sail line harder than was strictly necessary and tied it off, his heart pumping hard enough to blow a gasket.

He reprogrammed the autopilot. The maritime weather report had said they were in for a quiet day of smooth sailing.

Smooth sailing, my butt.

Not likely with Xanthe on board.

He'd wanted to bring the princess down a peg or two when she'd shown up on deck looking slim and beautiful and superior. He sure as hell wasn't going to let her sunbathe in front of him while he took the wheel like a lackey. Or that's how it had started. But the truth was he'd wanted her to wear the PFD, had decided to insist upon it, because he'd been unable to control the dumb urge to make sure she was safe.

And as soon as he'd had her in his arms again, yelling and punching as he carted her below deck, the desire to have her again had all but overwhelmed him too…

Then he'd lost it entirely when she'd made that crack about him wanting a piece of her precious company.

He hated that feeling—hated knowing she could still get to him. Knowing that there was something about Xanthe that could slip under his guard and make him care about her opinion when it shouldn't matter to him any more.

Resentment sat like a lead weight in his stomach.

From now on there was going to be no more sparring and no more conversations about their past. He wasn't going to get hung up on why she hadn't been sailing for ten years, even though she'd once been addicted to the rush. Or waste one more iota of his time getting mad about the fact she didn't trust him.

Their marriage was over—had been over for a long time—and it wasn't as if he wanted to resurrect it.

Arousal pulsed in his crotch, adding to his aggravation.

He usually averaged five hours' sleep a night when he was sailing solo, despite the need to wake up every twenty minutes and check the watch. Last night he hadn't managed more than two. Because he'd spent hours watching the stars wink in the darkness, thinking about all the stuff that might have been, while waiting for the night air to cool the heat powering through his body.

The only connection between them now was sexual, pure and simple—an animal attraction that had never died. Complicating that by sifting through all the baggage that had gone before would be a mistake.

So keeping Xanthe at arm's length for a little while

made sense—until he knew for sure that he could control all those wayward emotions she seemed able to provoke without even trying.

He doubted they'd be able to keep their hands off each other for the three days they had left together on the boat—but he could handle the heat until she got one thing straight.

Sex was the only thing he had to offer.

CHAPTER FOURTEEN

'DANE, IS EVERYTHING OKAY?' Xanthe yelled above the whistling wind as she clambered on deck and clipped her safety harness to an anchor point.

The yacht mounted another five-foot wave as water washed over the bow and the rain lashed her face.

Their argument over the life jacket yesterday seemed like a distant memory now.

'Get below, damn it, and stay there!' he shouted back, wrestling with the wheel to avoid a breaking wave— which brought with it the danger of capsizing.

The squall had hit with less than an hour's warning that morning. Dane had woken her up from a fitful sleep to issue some curt instructions about how to prepare the belowdecks, given her a quick drill on the emergency procedures if they had to use the life raft, insisted she take some seasickness pills and then ordered her to stay below.

After yesterday's argument and the evening that had followed—with the tension between them stretching tight as they both avoided each other as best they could—the rough weather and their clearly defined roles this morning had actually come as a relief.

So she'd obeyed his terse commands without question, even while smarting at his obvious determination not to give her anything remotely strenuous to do. When it came to skippering the boat, he was in charge. It would be foolish to dispute that, or distract him, when all his attention needed to be on keeping them afloat.

Correcting his 'princess' assumptions could wait until they got through this.

But as the hours had rolled by and the storm had got progressively worse she'd become increasingly concerned and frustrated by his dogged refusal to let her help. Thunder and lightning had been added to the hazards aboard as the squall had moved from a force-four to something closer to a force-eight by the afternoon, but through it all Dane had continued to insist she stay below.

Rather than have a full-blown argument, which would only make things more treacherous with the visibility at almost zero, she'd kept busy manning the bilge pump, rigging safety lines in the cabin and locking down the chart table when the contents had threatened to spill out. All the while trying to stay calm and focused and zone out the heaving noise outside.

They'd come through the worst of it an hour ago. The torrential rain was still flattening the seas, but the winds were dying down at least a little bit. But two seconds ago she'd heard a solid crash and she'd rushed up on deck, no longer prepared to follow orders.

Relief washed through her to see Dane standing at the wheel, the storm sails intact. But her relief quickly retreated.

His face was drawn, his clothing soaked, his usually graceful movements jerky and uncoordinated. He looked completely shattered. She cursed herself for waiting so long to finally confront him about his stubborn refusal to allow her on deck.

He'd been helming the yacht for over five hours and hadn't slept for more than twenty minutes at a time since they'd left Bermuda two days ago because he'd been keeping watch solo.

Maybe it had been ten years ago, but she'd once been a competent yachtswoman because she'd learnt from a master. She should take the helm. There weren't as many breakers to negotiate now, visibility was lifting and a quick survey of the horizon showed clear skies off the bow only a few miles ahead.

'Dane, for goodness' sake. Let me take over. You need some sleep.'

'Get back below, damn it!'

He swung the wheel to starboard and the boat heeled. But as she grabbed the safety line she saw a trickle of blood mixed with the rain running down his face, seeping from a gash at his hairline.

Horror gripped her insides, and her frustration was consumed by panic. 'Dane, you're bleeding!'

He scrubbed a forearm across his forehead. 'I'm okay.'

Hauling herself up to the stern, she covered his much larger hand with hers, shocked by the freezing skin as he clung to the wheel.

'This is insane,' she said, desperate now to make him see reason. 'I can *do* this. You have to let me do this.'

An involuntary shudder went through him, and she realised exactly how close he was to collapsing when he turned towards her, his blue eyes bloodshot and foggy with fatigue. Good grief, had he given himself a concussion?

'It's too rough still,' he said, the words thick with exhaustion. 'It's not safe for you up here.'

'It's a lot calmer than it was,' she said, registering the weary determination in his voice. However stupidly macho he was being by refusing to admit weakness, his determination to stay at the helm was born out of a desire to protect her.

'At least go below and clean the cut,' she said, clamping down on all the treacherous memories flooding back to make her heart ache.

The mornings when he'd held her head as she threw up her breakfast in the motel bathroom…the intractable look on his face when he'd demanded she marry him after the stick had gone blue…and the crippling thought of him battered and bruised by her father's bodyguards when he'd come back to get her…

Her gaze drifted over his brow to the scar that he'd refused to explain. She shook off the melancholy thoughts as blood seeped from the fresh injury on his forehead. She couldn't think about any of that now. He had a head injury. She had to get him to let go—at least for a little while.

'Seriously, I can handle this!' she shouted above the gusting wind, her voice firm and steady despite the memory bombarding her of another argument—the one they'd had the morning he'd left her…

She'd let him have the last word then, because she hadn't had the courage to insist she was capable of handling at least some of the burden of their finances. She'd been so angry about his attitude that morning, at his blank refusal to let her get a job.

But maybe it was finally time to acknowledge the truth of what had happened that day. *Of course* he'd had no faith in her abilities—because she'd had no faith in them herself. And he hadn't left her. He'd gone to find a job so he could support her.

He hadn't been able to rely on her because she *had* been weak and feeble, beaten down by her father's bullying. And her one show of strength—the decision to run off and marry Dane and have the baby growing inside her—had really been nothing more than a transference of power from one man to another.

Dane had made all the decisions simply because she'd been too scared, too unsure to make them herself. That Dane might have been equally scared, equally terrified, had never even occurred to her. But what if he had been? And what if he'd kept his feelings hidden simply to stop himself from scaring her?

'I'm not a princess any more, Dane!' she shouted, just in case he was still confusing her with that girl. She didn't want to argue with him, but she had to make him believe she could handle this. 'I'm a lot tougher than I look now,' she added.

Because I've had to be.

She cut off the thought. She could never tell him all the reasons why she'd been forced to toughen up because that would only stir up more of the guilt and recriminations from their past. Until she'd found herself alone in that motel bathroom she'd let him take all the strain. But she didn't need to do that any more.

'Please let me do this.'

She braced herself for an argument, keeping an eye on the sea, but to her astonishment, instead of arguing further, he grasped her arm and dragged her in front of him.

His big body bolstered hers and she felt the familiar zing of sexual awareness, complicated by a rush of emotion when his cold palms covered her hands on the wheel.

Tears stung her eyes and she blinked them away.

'You sure you can hold her?' he said, and the exhilaration in her chest combined with a lingering sense of loss for that complicated, taciturn boy who had taught her to sail a lifetime ago. And whom she had once loved without question.

She nodded.

He stood behind her, shielding her from the beating rain. She melted into him for a moment and the punch of adrenaline hit her square in the solar plexus, taking her breath away as she felt the boat's power beneath her feet.

When she'd been that frightened, insecure girl, scared of her father's wrath, always looking for his approval, Dane had given her this—the freedom and space to become her own woman. And she'd screwed it up by falling for him hook, line and sinker.

If this time with him taught her one thing, let it be that she would never do that again. Never look for love when what she really needed was strength.

'Go below! I've got this!' she shouted over her shoulder, trying to concentrate on the job at hand and not let all the what-ifs charging through her head destroy the simple companionship of this moment.

'I won't be long,' he said, and the husky words sprinted up her spine.

Giving her fingers a reassuring squeeze, he took a deep breath and stepped away, leaving her alone at the helm. He pointed towards the horizon.

'Head towards the clear blue. And avoid the breakers.'

She concentrated on the break in the storm line, scanning the sea for the next wave. 'Will do. Take as long as you need.'

Widening her stance, she let her limbs absorb the heel of the boat as it rode over the swell. The rain was finally starting to trail off. Arousal leapt, combining with the deep well of emotion, as she watched him unclip himself from the safety line and saw his shoulders fill the entryway before he disappeared below.

The boat rolled to the side and Dane's heart went with it, kicking against his ribs like a bucking bronco as he staggered into the salon, his head hurting like a son of a bitch, but his heart hurting more.

He shook his hands and the shivering racked his body as he stripped off the life jacket and the wet clothing with clumsy fingers and headed back to his cabin.

He didn't want to leave Xanthe alone up there too long. She'd always been a natural sailor, and he'd sensed a new toughness and tenacity in her now, a greater resilience than when they were kids together. But even so she was his responsibility while she was on the boat, and he didn't want to screw it up. *Again.*

He winced as shame engulfed him. He'd already put her at risk, sailing them both straight into a force-eight because he'd been too damn busy thinking about the hot, wet clasp of her body and trying to decipher all the conflicting emotions she could still stir in him, instead of paying the necessary attention to the weather report, the cloud formation and the sudden dip in air pressure.

They'd been lucky that it hadn't been a whole lot worse.

But he knew when he was beaten. He had to sleep— get a good solid thirty minutes before he could relieve her at the helm. Gripping the safety line she'd rigged, he made his way to the head, dug out a piece of gauze to dab the cut on his forehead, then staggered naked into the cabin.

Thirty minutes—that was all he needed—then he'd be able to take over again.

His eyes closed, and his brain shut off the minute his head connected with the pillow.

He woke with a start what felt like moments later, to find the cabin dark and the boat steady. The events of the day—the last few days—came back in a rush.

Xanthe.

He jerked upright and pain lanced through the cut on his forehead where he'd headbutted the boom. He cursed. How long had he been out? He'd forgotten to set an alarm before crashing into his berth. He looked up to see clear night through the skylight. Then noticed the blanket lying across his lap.

The blanket that hadn't been there when he'd fallen headlong into the bunk what had to be *hours* ago.

Emotion gripped as he pulled the blanket off.

Was she still on deck? Doing his job for him?

Ignoring the dull pain in his head, he pulled on some trunks and a light sweater. Heading through the salon, he noticed the debris left by the storm had been cleared away and the film of water that had leaked in through the hatch onto the floor had been mopped up. His wet clothes hung on the safety line, brittle with salt but nearly dry.

The night breeze lifted the hairs on his arms as he climbed onto the deck. The helm was empty, the autopilot was on, the storm sails were furled and the standard rigging was engaged as the boat coasted on a shallow swell.

Xanthe lay curled up in the cockpit, out cold, her PFD still anchored to the safety line, her fist clutching the alarm clock.

His heart hammered hard enough to hurt his bruised ribs.

He cast his gaze out to sea, where the red light of a Caribbean dawn hung on the horizon, and struggled to breathe past the emotion making his chest ache.

She'd seen them through the last of the storm, then kept watch all night while he slept. How could someone who looked so delicate, so fragile, be so strong underneath? And what the hell did he do with all the feelings weak-

ening his knees now? Feelings he'd thought he had conquered a decade ago?

Desire, possessiveness, and a bone-deep longing.

He'd convinced himself a long time ago that Xanthe
had never really belonged to him. That what he'd felt for
her once had all been a dumb dream driven by endorphins and recklessness and desperation. He didn't want
to be that needy kid again. So why did this feel like more
than just the desire to bury himself deep inside her?

He crouched down on his haunches, forcing the traitorous feelings back.

He was still tired—and more than a little horny after
three days at sea with the one woman he had never
been able to resist. It had been an emotional couple of
days. And the storm had been a sucker punch neither
of them had needed.

He pressed his hand to her cheek, pushing the wild
hair, damp with sea water, off her brow. She stirred, and
the bronco in his chest gave his ribs another hefty kick.

'Hmm...?' Her eyes fluttered open, the sea green
dazed with sleep. 'Dane?' she murmured, licking her
lips.

The blood flowed into his groin and he welcomed
it. Sex had always been the easy part of the equation.

'Hey, sleepyhead,' he said, affection and admiration
swelling in his chest.

This wasn't a big deal. She'd done a spectacular job
and he owed her—that was all. Unclipping her harness,
he lifted her easily in his arms.

'Let's get you below. I can take over now.' The way
he should have done approximately twelve hours ago.

He realised how groggy she was when she didn't protest as he carried her down the steps into the salon and headed to his own cabin.

He wanted her in his bed while he took charge of the boat. By his calculation they'd reach the Bahamas around twilight. They'd have to anchor offshore, and dock first thing tomorrow morning, but he intended to keep his hands off her for the rest of the trip. Even if it killed him.

Then he'd sign her divorce papers.

And let her go.

Before this situation got any more out of hand.

Sitting her on the bed, he crouched down to undo her jacket. She didn't resist his attentions, docile as a child as he pulled it off and chucked it on the floor. Her T-shirt was stuck to her skin, the hard tips of her nipples clear through the clinging fabric.

He gritted his teeth, ignoring the pounding in his groin. The desire to warm those cold nubs with his tongue almost overwhelming.

'How's your head?' she murmured sleepily.

He glanced up to find her watching him, her gaze unfocused, dark with arousal.

'Good,' he said, his voice strained.

She needed to get out of her wet clothes, grab a hot shower. But if he did it for her he didn't know how the heck he'd be able to keep his sanity and not take advantage of her.

'Have you got it from here?'

He tugged the clock out of his back pocket. Fifteen minutes before he had to check the watch.

'I should head back on deck,' he said, hoping she couldn't see the erection starting to strangle in his shorts. Or hear the battle being waged inside him to hold her and tend to her and claim her again...

Because he knew if that happened he might never be able to let her go.

Sleep fogged Xanthe's brain, as her mind floated on a wave of exhaustion. He looked glorious, standing before her in the half-light—the epitome of all the erotic dreams which had chased her through too many nights of disturbed sleep. Strong and unyielding... The raw, rugged beauty of his tanned skin, his muscular shoulders, the dark heat in his pure blue eyes, blazed a trail down to tighten her nipples into aching points.

She shivered, awareness shuddering through her.

She heard a strained curse, then the bed dipped and her T-shirt was dragged over her head. The damp shorts and underwear followed. Her limbs were lethargic, her skin tingling as calloused fingers rasped over sensitive flesh with exquisite tenderness, beckoning her further into the erotic dream and making her throat close.

'Red, you're freezing...let's warm you up.'

She found herself back in strong arms, her body weightless. But she didn't feel cold. She felt blissfully warm and languid, with hunger flaring all over her tired body as she stood on shaky legs.

Hot jets of water rained down on her head as strong fingers massaged her scalp. She breathed in the scented steam—cedarwood and lemon—her body alive with sensation as a fluffy towel cocooned her in warmth, making her feel clean and fresh, the vigorous rubbing igniting more of that ravishing heat.

Back on the bed, she looked into that rugged face watching her in the darkness, its expression tight with a longing that matched her own.

Struggling up onto her elbows, she traced a finger through the hair on his chest, naked now, down the happy trail through the rigid muscles of his abdomen to his belly button.

She heard him suck in a staggered breath, and the sound was both warning and provocation. Emotion washed through her as she stroked the heavy ridge in his pants and felt the huge erection thicken against her fingertips.

A hand gripped her wrist and gently pulled her away. 'Red, you're killing me,' he murmured, his low voice raw with agony.

She lifted her head, saw the harsh need that pierced her abdomen reflected in Dane's deep blue eyes. Drifting in a sensual haze, she let the uncensored swell of emotion fill up all the places in her heart that had been empty for so long.

'Stay with me.'

The words came out on a husk of breath, almost unrecognisable. Was that *her* voice? So sure, so uninhibited, so determined?

'I need you.'

A tiny whisper in her head told her it was wrong to ask, wrong to need him this much. But this was just a dream, a dream from long ago, and nothing mattered now but satisfying the yearning which had begun to cut off her air supply and stab into her abdomen like a knife.

'There's never been anyone else,' she said. 'Only you. Don't make me beg.'

Moisture stung her eyes—tears of pain and sadness for all those dreams that had been forced to die inside her, along with the life they'd once made together. If she could just feel that glorious oblivion once more all would be well.

Only he could fix this.

'Shh... Shh, Red...' Rough palms framed her face, swiping away the salty tears seeping from her eyes. 'I've got this. Lie down and I'll give you what you need.'

She flopped back on the bed, then bowed up, racked with pleasure as his tongue circled her nipples, firm lips tugging at the tender tips. Desire arrowed down. Sharp and brutal. Obliterating every emotion but want.

Moisture flooded between her thighs as blunt fingers found the swollen folds of her sex. Her breath sawed out, her lungs squeezing tight as the agony of loss was swept away by the fierce tide of ecstasy.

She bucked, cried out, as those sure, seeking lips trailed across her ribs, delved into her belly button, then found the swollen bundle of nerves at last. Sensation shot through her, drawing tight, clutching at her heart and firing through her nerve-endings, making everything disappear but the agonising need to feel him filling her again.

Large fingers pressed inside her and her clitoris burned and pulsed under the sensual torment. The wave of ecstasy crested, throwing her into the hot, dark oblivion she sought. She screamed his name, the cry of joy dying on her lips as she tasted her own pleasure in a hard, fleeting kiss.

'Now, go to sleep.'

She registered the gruff command, making her feel safe and cherished.

His hand cradled her face and she pressed into his palm, the gentle touch making new tears spill over her lids as she closed her eyes. A blanket fell over her and she snuggled into a ball, drifting on an enervating wave of afterglow.

And then she dived into a deep, dreamless sleep.

CHAPTER FIFTEEN

'Is THAT NASSAU?' Xanthe called out to Dane, hoping the flush on her face wasn't as bright as the lights she could see across the bay, which had to be the commercial and cultural capital of the Bahamas.

A kaleidoscope of red and orange hues painted the sky where the sun dipped beneath a silhouette of palm trees and colourful waterfront shacks on the nearby beach.

She'd slept the whole day away. Her body felt limber and alive, well-rested and rejuvenated… Unfortunately that wasn't doing anything for her peace of mind as snatches of conversation from the hour before dawn, when Dane had come to relieve her on deck after her shattering stint at the helm, made her heart pummel her chest and her face burn with the heat of a thousand suns.

Had she actually begged him to give her an orgasm?

Yup, she was pretty sure she had.

And had she blurted out that he'd been the only man she'd ever slept with?

Way to go, Xanthe.

How exactly did she come back from that with any

dignity? Especially as she could still feel the phantom stroke of his tongue on her clitoris?

He stopped what he was doing with the rigging and strolled across the deck towards her.

The fluid gait, sure-footed and purposeful and naturally predatory, put all her senses on high alert and turned the tingle in her clitoris to a definite hum.

'Yeah, the marina is on Paradise Island,' he said as he approached, his deep voice reverberating through her sternum. 'But we're anchored here till morning. It's too dangerous to try docking after sunset.'

The blush became radioactive as he studied her face. 'You slept okay?'

'Yes... Thank you.' Like the dead, for twelve solid hours.

The memory of him washing her hair, rubbing her naked skin with a towel and then blasting away all her other aches and pains made her heart jam her larynx.

'You're welcome.' His lips kicked up on one side, the sensual curve making the pit of her stomach sink into the toes of her deck shoes. 'Thanks for taking such good care of *The Sea Witch*,' he murmured.

Her knees trembled, her heart swelling painfully in her throat at the thought of how carefully he'd taken care of *her*.

Who was she kidding? This wasn't just about sex—not any more. Or at least not for her. The fear she thought she'd ridden into the dust kicked back up under her breastbone. She was falling for him again. And she didn't seem to be able to stop herself.

His gaze glided over the blush now setting fire to her cheeks.

'Is there a problem?' he asked.

She cleared her throat.

Backing down had never been the answer with Dane—she of all people ought to know that by now. Being coy or embarrassed now would be suicidal.

He'd left her feeling fragile and vulnerable and scared. Which almost certainly hadn't been his intention, because having her love him had never been part of Dane's agenda. She had to turn this around, make it clear that sex was the only thing they still shared... Or he'd know exactly how much last night had meant to her.

'Actually there is, and it has to do with your extremely altruistic use of your superpower,' she said, cutting straight to the chase.

His eyebrows hiked up his forehead.

'And how is that a problem?' he asked, but it wasn't really a question. The bite of sarcasm was unmistakable.

She'd annoyed him. This was good.

'Not a problem, exactly,' she said—as if she could dispute that, when he'd turned her into a quivering mess who had screamed his name out at top volume. 'But I would have been fine without it. I didn't need a pity orgasm.'

'A... A pity *what*?' Dane choked on the words as the tension in his gut gripped the base of his spine and turned his insides into a throbbing knot of need. 'What the *hell* are you talking about?'

'I didn't need you to take pity on me. When I said I

wanted to make love to you, I planned to hold up my end of the bargain.'

'How?'

Anger surged through him. He'd been on a knife-edge all damn day, his emotions in turmoil, his hunger for her driving him nuts—but not nearly as much as his yearning to ask her to stay with him. Which was even more nuts. They'd grown up, gone their separate ways. They had nothing in common now—nothing that should make him want her this much. And now she was accusing him of... What?

He didn't even know what she was talking about. He'd given her the one thing he was capable of giving her without sinking them both any further into the mire. And she'd just told him she hadn't wanted that either.

'You were exhausted—barely awake,' he ground out. 'Because you'd been up all night doing *my* damn job for me.' Blood was pulsing into his crotch, making it hard for him to regulate his temper. Or his voice, which had risen to a shout they could probably hear back in Manhattan. 'You needed to sleep.'

Her cheeks flushed. 'So you decided to help me with that? Well, thanks a bunch. Next time I have insomnia I'll be sure to order up Dane's pity orgasm remedy.'

'You ungrateful little witch.'

Fury overwhelmed him. He'd wanted nothing more than to feel her come apart in his arms, make her moan and beg and say his name and *only* his name. But she'd been tired and emotional. And then she'd struck him right through the heart with that statement about him being the only one.

It had taken him a moment to figure out what she was telling him. But when he'd got it—when he'd realised he was the only guy she'd ever slept with—it had felt like watching his boat shoot across the finishing line of the America's Cup and being knifed in the gut all at the same time.

The burst of pride and pleasure and possessiveness had combined with the terror of wanting to hold on to her too much—throwing him all the way back to the grinding fear of his childhood. So he'd held back. He'd given her what she needed without taking what he wanted for himself.

And now she was telling him what he'd given her wasn't enough.

'Ungrateful?' She seared him with a look that could have cut through lead. 'Don't you get it? I don't *want* to be grateful. I'm not a charity case. I want to be your equal. In bed as well as out of it.'

He grabbed her arms, dragged her close. 'You want to participate this time? I don't have a problem with that.'

She thrust her hands into his hair, digging her fingers into the short strands to haul his mouth to within a whisper of hers. The desire sparking in her eyes turned the mossy green to emerald fire.

'Good, because neither do I,' she said, then planted her lips on his.

The kiss went from wild to insane in a heartbeat. The need that had been churning in his gut all day surged out of control as he boosted her into his arms.

He couldn't keep her, but he could sure as hell ensure she never forgot him.

* * *

Rough stubble abraded Xanthe's palms as her whole body sang the 'Hallelujah Chorus.' Her breasts flattened against his chest and their mouths duelled in a wild, uncontrollable battle for supremacy.

His tongue thrust deep, dominant and demanding, parrying with hers as wildfire burned through her system. She hooked her legs round his waist, clinging on as he staggered down to the cabin with her wrapped around him like a limpet.

Barging through the door, he flung her onto the bed. She lurched onto her knees, watching as he kicked off his trunks. The thick erection bounced free, hard and long and ready for her.

Everything inside her melted. All the anger and agony and the terrifying vulnerability was flushed away on a wave of longing so intense she thought she might pass out.

This was all they had ever been able to have. She had to remember that.

He grabbed the front of her T-shirt and hauled her up, ripping the thin cotton down the middle. His lips crushed hers, his tongue claiming her mouth again in a soul-numbing kiss. Drawing back, he helped her struggle out of the rest of her clothing, his groans matched by the pants of her breathing.

At last they were naked, the feel of his skin warm and firm, tempered by the steely strength beneath. Muscles rippled with tension beneath her stroking palms. He cupped her sex, his fingers finding the heart of her with unerring accuracy. She bucked off the bed, his touch too much for her tender flesh. He circled with his thumb, knowing just how to caress her, to draw out her pleasure to breaking point. His lips clamped to a nipple and drew it deep into his mouth.

Sensations collided, then crashed through her. She sobbed as the blistering climax hit—hard and fast and not enough.

'I need you inside me,' she sobbed, desperate to forget about the aching emptiness that had tormented her for so long.

He rose up, grasped her hips, positioned himself to plunge deep. But as he pressed at her entrance he froze suddenly. Then dropped his forehead to hers and swore loudly. 'I don't have any protection. This wasn't supposed to happen.'

His dark gaze met hers, and her brutal arousal was reflected in those blindingly blue eyes. She blurted out the truth. 'It's okay. As long as we're both clean. I won't get pregnant.'

'You're on the pill?'

The gruff assumption reached inside her and ripped open the gaping wound she'd spent years denying even existed. She slammed down on the wrenching pain. And on the urge to tell him the terrible truth of how much she'd lost by loving him.

Don't tell him. You can't.

'Yes,' she lied.

He kissed her, his groan of relief echoing in her sternum, feeding her own need back to her. Then he angled her hips and thrust deep.

Her body arched, and the sensation of fullness was

overwhelming as she struggled to adjust to the thick intrusion. He began to move, driving into her in a devastating rhythm that dug at that spot inside only he had ever touched.

'Let go, Red. I want to see you come again. Just for me.'

The possessive tone, the desperation in his demand felt too real, too frightening. She'd given him everything once. She couldn't afford to give it all to him again.

'I can't.'

'Yes, you can.' He found her clitoris with his thumb. Swollen and aching.

The perfect touch drove her back towards the peak with staggering speed. Her whole body clamped down, euphoria driving through the fear. His eyes met hers, the intensity in their blue depths reaching out and touching her heart.

She gripped broad shoulders, the muscles tensed beneath her fingertips as she tried to shield herself against the intense wave of emotion. But it rose up anyway, shaking her to the core as her body soared past that last barrier to plunge into the abyss.

He shouted out, the sound muffled against her neck, as he emptied his seed into her womb.

She came to moments later, his body heavy on hers. The bright, beautiful wave of afterglow receded, to be replaced by the shattering feeling of an emotion she hadn't wanted to feel.

Lifting up on his elbows, he brushed the hair back

from her brow. The shuttered look in his eyes made her shudder with reaction. The feeling of him still intimately linked to her was too much.

'Are you okay?' he said.

The wariness in his expression made her heart feel heavy. How could he protect himself so easily when she'd never been able to protect herself in return?

One rough palm caressed her cheek and she turned away from it, feeling the sting of tears behind her eyelids at this glimpse of tenderness.

This was just sex for him. That was all it had ever been.

'Never better.' She pressed her palms against his chest, suddenly feeling trapped. And fragile. 'I need to clean up.'

He rolled off her without complaint. But as she tried to scramble off the bed firm fingers caught her wrist, holding her in place. 'Xan, don't.'

She glanced over her shoulder. 'Don't what?'

'Don't run off.'

He tugged her back towards him and slung an arm around her shoulder, and—weak and feeble woman that she was—she let him draw her under his arm until her head was nestled against his chest, her palm resting over his heart, which was still beating double time with hers.

His thumb caressed her cheek, and the rumble of his voice in her ear drew her in deeper. 'Why has there never been anyone else?'

She considered denying it. If he'd sounded smug or arrogant she probably would have, but all he sounded was guarded.

'I wish I hadn't told you that.' She sighed. 'It was a weak moment. Can't you forget it?'

'Nope,' he murmured into her hair.

It occurred to her that he probably didn't want *this* burden any more than he'd wanted any of the others she'd thrust upon him.

'If it's any consolation,' he said, his fingers threading through her hair as his deep voice rumbled against her ear, 'there hasn't been anyone important for me either.'

Her heartbeat hitched into an uneven rhythm. Ten years ago that admission would have had her bursting with happiness. She would have taken it as a sign. A sign that she meant something to him. Something beyond the obvious. But she wasn't that optimistic any more. Or as much of a pushover. And she couldn't risk letting herself believe again. Because it had already cost her far too much.

'I guess we've both been pretty busy...' She tried to smile, but the crooked tilt of her lips felt weak and forced.

'I guess,' he said.

The husky agreement let them both off the hook. Until he spoke again.

'That scar—low under your belly button. How did you get it?'

She stilled, unable to talk, struggling to stop her eyes filling with unshed tears.

'Was it the baby?'

The hint of hesitation in his voice made her heart pound even harder, emotion closing her throat.

She nodded.

His arm tightened.

She needed to talk about this. To tell him all the things she'd been robbed of the chance to tell him then.

Perhaps this was why it had always felt as if there was more between them? She clung to the thought. So much of their past remained unresolved. Maybe if she took this opportunity to remedy that they could go their separate ways without so many regrets?

All she had to do was get enough breath into her lungs to actually speak.

Dane's heart thudded against his collarbone. He could feel the tension in her body, her silent struggle to draw a full breath. He'd known it had been bad for her. He hadn't meant to bring all that agony back. But the question had slipped out, his desire to know as desperate as his desire to comfort her. And for once his anger at her father was nowhere near as huge as his anger with himself.

Whatever the old bastard had done after the fact, Dane was the one who'd stormed out of that motel room and hadn't contacted her for days.

So when all was said and done it was down to him that he hadn't been there when she'd needed him. However much he had tried to put the blame on her old man.

'Can you talk about it?' he asked, the husk of his voice barely audible.

She nodded again and cleared her throat. The raw sound scraped over his temper and dug into the guilt beneath. When her voice finally came it wasn't loud, but it was steady.

'I have a scar because they had to operate. I was bleeding heavily and they...'

She hesitated for a moment, and the slight hitch in her breathing was like a knife straight into his heart.

'They couldn't get a heartbeat.'

Hell.

He settled his hand on her head, tugged her closer. The urge to lend her his strength impossible to deny, however useless it might be now.

'I'm so damn sorry, Red. I should never have insisted on marrying you and taking you to that damn motel. It was a dive. You would have been okay if you'd stayed on daddy's estate...'

She pulled out of his arms, her eyes fierce and full of raw feeling as she silenced him with a finger across his lips.

'Stop it!'

Her voice sounded choked. And he could see the sheen of tears in her eyes, crucifying him even more.

'That's not true. It would have happened regardless. And I wanted to be with *you*.'

He captured her finger, his heart battering his ribs so hard now he was astonished that it didn't jump right out of his chest.

'He was right about me, though,' he said.

'What was he right about?' She seemed puzzled—as if she really didn't get it.

'He called me a wharf rat. And that's exactly what I was.'

He pushed the words out, and tried to feel relieved

that he'd finally told her the truth. The one thing he'd been so desperate to keep from her all those years ago.

'I grew up in a trailer park that was one step away from being the town dump. My old man was a drunk who got his kicks from beating the crap out of me, so I hung around the marina to get away from him until I got big enough to hit back.'

Even if the squalid truth about who he really was and where he'd come from could never undo all the stuff he'd done wrong, at least it would go some way to show her how truly sorry he was—for all the pain he'd caused.

'If that doesn't make me a wharf rat, I don't know what does.'

Xanthe clutched the sheet covering her breasts, which were heaving now as if she'd just run a marathon. Her mind reeled from Dane's statement. So it *was* his father who had caused those terrible scars on his back. She'd always suspected as much. Sympathy twisted in her stomach—not just for that boy, but for the look in Dane's eyes now that told her he actually *believed* what he was saying.

How could she have got it so wrong? She had believed his silence about himself and his past had been the result of arrogance and pride and indifference, when what it had really been was defensiveness.

'I'm sorry your father hurt you like that.'

And what did she do with the evidence that it still hurt her so much to know he'd been abused?

'Don't feel sorry for that little bastard,' he said. 'He didn't deserve it.'

Of course he did. But how could she tell him that without giving away the truth—that a part of her had never stopped loving that boy.

'My father called you a wharf rat because he was an unconscionable snob, Dane. It had nothing to do with you.' That much at least she could tell him.

'He loved you, Xan, and he wanted to protect you. There's nothing wrong with that,' he said with a weary resignation. 'If I could have…' His gaze strayed to her belly and the thin white scar left behind by the surgeon's incision. 'I would have protected our baby the same way.'

The admission cut through her, and emotions that were already far too close to the surface threatened to spill over.

God, how could she have accused him of not caring about their child when it was obvious now that he might have cared too much? Enough to blame himself for the things that her father—both their fathers—had done.

She bit down on the feelings threatening to choke her.

'That's where you're wrong. He didn't love me. He thought of me as his property.'

How come she had never acknowledged that until now? All those years she'd worked her backside off to please her father, to get his approval, never once questioning what he had ever done to deserve it.

'I was an investment. The daughter who was going to marry a man of *his* choosing who would take over Carmichael's when he was gone. My falling in love… having a child by a man he disapproved of and who re-

fused to bow down to the mighty Charles Carmichael…
they were the real reasons he hated you.'

Dane cupped her cheek, the cool touch making her
heart ache even more.

'I guess we both got a raw deal when the good Lord
gave out daddies.'

She let out a half laugh, and the tears that had refused
to fall for so long threatened to cascade over her lids.

She settled back into his arms, so he wouldn't see
them. 'The baby was a little boy,' she said, determined
to concentrate on their past and not on their future, because they didn't have one.

'For real?'

She heard awe as well as sadness in his tone.

'I thought you should know.'

Their baby, after all, was the only thing that had
brought them together. Surely this chance to say goodbye to him properly would finally allow them to part.

'I'm glad you told me,' he murmured, his fingers
linking with hers, his thumb rubbing over her wrist
where her pulse hammered.

She hiccupped, her breath hurting again, the tears
flowing freely down her cheeks now.

'Hell, Red, don't cry,' he said, kissing the top of her
head and gathering her close. 'It's all over now.'

She splayed her fingers over the solid mass of his
pectoral muscles, feeling exhausted and hollowed out.
Because she knew it *wasn't* over. Not for her. And she was
becoming increasingly terrified that it never had been.

CHAPTER SIXTEEN

XANTHE WOKE THE following morning feeling tired and confused.

Dane had woken her twice in the night. The skill and urgency of his lovemaking had been impossible to resist. He'd caught her unawares, that clever thumb stroking her to climax while she was still drifting on dreams… She stretched, feeling the aches and pains caused by the energy of their lovemaking.

Last night's revelations had been painful for them both, but getting that glimpse of the boy she'd once known and finally knowing more of what had haunted him felt important.

The boat swayed and she heard a bump. Glancing out of the window, she could see the masts of another boat. They had arrived at the marina on Paradise Island.

Getting out of bed, she slung on capri pants and one of Dane's T-shirts and poured herself a cup of coffee from the pot Dane had already brewed. As she loaded it up with cream and sugar she tried to deal with all the confusing emotions spiralling through her system.

She was in trouble. Big trouble. That much was obvious. And it wasn't just a result of last night's confidences, the hot sex, or even the tumultuous day spent battling the elements together. This problem went right back to her decision a week ago to bring Dane those divorce papers in person.

Every single decision she'd made since had proved one thing. However smart and focused and rational and sensible she thought she'd become in the last ten years, and however determined never to let any man have control over her life, one man always had. And she'd been in denial about it.

But she wasn't that fanciful girl any more—that girl who had loved too easily and without discrimination. She was a grown woman who knew the score. She had to bring that maturity to bear now.

She poured the dregs of her barely touched coffee down the sink.

Taking a deep but unsteady breath, she headed up on deck. Dane stood on the dock, tall and indomitable and relaxed, talking to a younger man in board shorts and a bill cap. Her heart jolted as it had so often in the past, but this time she didn't try to deny the profound effect he had on her.

He'd shaved, revealing the delicious dent in his chin which she could remember licking last night.

She shook off the erotic thought.

Not helping.

Dane spotted her standing on the deck and broke off his conversation. His hot gaze skimmed down her body as he walked towards her.

'Morning,' he said.

'Hi.'

She stood her ground as he climbed onto the boat, the heat in his eyes sending her senses reeling.

'I should head home today,' she said, as casually as she could, and held her breath, waiting for any flicker of acknowledgement that what had happened last night was a big deal. 'I thought I'd check out the flights from Nassau.'

She silently cursed the way her heart clenched at his patient perusal.

'Why don't you stay for one more night?' he said at last. 'I've got a suite booked at the Paradise Resort before I head back to Manhattan tomorrow.'

She sank her hands into the back pockets of her capri pants to stop them trembling and control the sweet hit of adrenaline kicking under her breastbone. What was making her so giddy? It was hardly a declaration of undying love.

'Why would you want to do that?' she asked, determined to accept the casual invitation in the spirit it was offered.

He gave her a long look, and for a terrible moment she thought he could see what she was trying so hard to hide—the panic, the longing, and all those foolish dreams which had failed to die.

But then his lips lifted in a sensual smile and heat fired down to her core. 'Because we've both been through hell in the last couple of days and I figure we've earned a reward.'

He touched a knuckle to her cheek, skimmed it down

to touch the throbbing pulse in her neck. The snap and crackle of sexual awareness went haywire.

'I could show you the town,' he added. 'Nassau's a cool city.'

'But I don't have anything to wear,' she said, still trying to weigh her options.

This wasn't a big deal. After the enforced intimacy of the boat, the intensity of emotion brought on by the storm, not to mention the lack of sleep and the stresses and strains of what had happened so long ago still hanging between them, why shouldn't he suggest one more night of fun? After all, they'd had precious little fun in their acquaintance. She had to take this at face value. Not read more into it than was actually there.

'You're not going to need much,' he said, his smile loaded with sensual promise. 'I was kidding about showing you around. We probably won't get out of the suite.'

She laughed, the wicked look in his eyes going some way to relieve the tension. 'What happens to *The Sea Witch* once you've gone back to Manhattan?' She glanced back at the boat, feeling a little melancholy at the thought of leaving it.

He nodded towards the young man still standing on the dock. 'Joe's my delivery skipper—he'll take it back to Boston.'

His hand cupped the back of her neck, sending sensation zinging all over her body.

'Now, quit stalling—do we have a deal or don't we?'

She swallowed heavily, her heart thudding against her throat. She could say no. She probably *should* say no. But having his gaze searching her face, his expression tense as he waited for her answer… She knew she didn't want to say no.

The man was intoxicating…like a dangerously addictive drug. She needed to be careful—conscious of all the emotions that had tripped her up in the past—but she was a stronger, wiser woman now, not a seventeen-year-old girl. And while she was riding the high had there ever been anything more exhilarating?

He tugged her into his arms, his lips inches from hers, the fire in his eyes incendiary. 'Say yes, Red. You know you want to.'

'Yes,' she whispered.

His lips covered hers and she let the leap of arousal mask the idiotic burst of optimism telling her that this might be more than she'd hoped it could be.

'Slow down, Dane. I'm stuffed. I don't want to burst the seams on this dress.'

Xanthe tried to sound stern as Dane clasped her hand and led her past the quaint, brightly coloured storefronts of Nassau's downtown area. The colonnades and verandas announced the island city's colonial heritage, while SUVs vied for space on the tourist-choked streets with horse-drawn carriages.

After four days on the yacht, the four-course meal in the luxurious surroundings of a Michelin-starred restaurant had been sensational, but the truth was she'd barely managed to swallow a bite. The potent hunger in his eyes every time he looked at her had turned her insides to mush.

She'd been riding a wave of endorphins since their bargain on the boat—but was determined not to let his invitation get the better of her. Then something had shifted when he had appeared in their enormous suite at the resort on Paradise Island looking breathtakingly handsome in a dark evening suit and told her he was taking her out on a date.

After all the sex they'd shared the suggestion shouldn't have seemed so sweet. So intimate. So overwhelming. But somehow it had.

'And you bursting out of your dress is supposed to be a problem?'

His eyes dipped to the hem of the designer dress she'd picked from the array of garments he'd had sent up to their suite. The incendiary gaze seared the skin of her thighs, already warmed by the Caribbean night.

'It *is* on a public street,' she shot back, struggling to quell the erratic beat of her heart.

The evening had been a revelation in some ways— Dane had played the gentleman with remarkable ease— but it had been only more disturbing in others.

Because getting a glimpse into his life now, and seeing the level of luxury he could afford, had only made her more aware of how far he'd come. He'd always been tenacious and determined, but she couldn't help her fierce wave of pride at the thought of how hard he'd worked to leave that boy behind and escape the miserable poverty of his childhood.

She shouldn't have been surprised by the exclusiveness of the five-star resort hotel on Paradise Island, or by the lavish bungalow that looked out onto a private white sand beach and the sleek black power boat he'd piloted to take them into Nassau—especially after seeing the penthouse apartment Dane owned in Manhattan—but, like Nassau itself, which was a heady mix of old world elegance, new world commerce and Caribbean laissez-faire, Dane seemed like a complex contradiction.

His animal magnetism was not dimmed in the slightest by this new layer of wealth and sophistication. Even in an elegant tuxedo, the raw, rugged masculinity of the man still shone through. The tailored jacket stretched tight over wide shoulders now, as he led her back towards the dock where the speedboat was moored.

'I've always thought clothes are overrated,' he teased, helping her into the boat. 'Especially on you.'

He shrugged off the jacket and dumped it in the back of the boat, then tugged off the tie, too, and stuffed it into the pocket of his suit trousers.

'I don't care how damn fancy that restaurant is,' he said, and the vehemence in his tone was surprising. 'Nothing's worth getting trussed-up like a chicken for.'

'You didn't like the food?' she asked.

'The food was great—but it was way too stuffy in there.'

He smiled at her, and the glint of white against his swarthy skin was a potent reminder of the boy. Wicked and reckless and hungry—for so much.

But was he hungry for *her*? In anything other than the most basic way?

He switched on the engine and the boat roared to life, kicking at the soft swell as he directed the boat away from the dock and into the water.

She glanced back at the fading lights of Bay Street, the wind pulling tendrils of hair out of her chignon as Dane handled the powerful boat with ease. And tried not to let the question torture her.

She mustn't get ahead of herself—read too much into this night.

She was concentrating so hard on getting everything into perspective that she didn't register that they weren't returning to the resort until the boat slowed as it approached a beach on the opposite side of the bay. A cluster of fairy lights and the bass beat of music covered by the lilting rumble of laughter and conversation announced a bar in the distance.

Dane released the throttle and let the boat drift into a small wooden dock lit by torches. Jumping out, he secured the line.

'Where are we?' she asked accepting his outstretched hand as he hauled her off the boat.

'An old hang-out of mine,' he said as she stepped onto the worn uneven boards.

He tugged her into his arms. Awareness sizzled through her system, but alongside it was the brutal tug of something more. Something that made her feel young and carefree and cherished—something she had been certain she would never feel again.

'I'm taking you dancing,' he said.

'You…? Really…?' Her breath choked off in her throat, and the panicked leap of her heart was almost as scary as the thundering beat of her pulse.

Was this another coincidence? Like the name of the boat? Surely it had to be.

But the wonder of the only other time they'd been dancing echoed in her heart regardless. The dark shapes of the cars in the car park…the strains of a country and Western band coming from the bar where they'd been refused entry when they'd spotted Dane's fake ID… Dane's strong arms directing her movements as he'd shown her the intricate steps and counter-steps of a Texas line dance and they'd laughed together every time she stepped on his toes.

And the giddy rush of adoration as they eventually settled into a slow dance on the cracked asphalt.

She'd been so hopelessly in love with him then.

She tried to thrust the memory aside as he led her down the dock, and ignored the swoop of her heart as he swung her into his arms to cross the sand.

She let out a laugh, though, desperate to live in the moment. Was this fate, testing her resolve?

Surely it was just the Caribbean evening, the promise of dancing the night away with such a forceful, stimulating man again and all the hot sex that lay in their immediate future that was making her as giddy as a teenager.

Dane's thoughts and feelings were still an enigma. And *her* thoughts and feelings had matured. She mustn't invest too much until she knew more.

She clung on to her resolve as he held her close in the moonlight, igniting her senses as they bumped and ground together to the sound of the vintage reggae band.

But as he guided the boat back towards Paradise Island her heart battered her ribcage, and excitement burst inside her like a firework when he murmured, 'I hope that made up for our wedding night.'

So he had remembered that treasured memory of dancing in the parking lot, too.

As they entered the suite he banded an arm round her waist and hauled her into his body.

'That's got to be the longest evening of my life.'

Breathing in the scent of salt and cedarwood soap which clung to him like a potent aphrodisiac, she spread her hands over his six-pack, felt his abs tense as arousal slammed into her system. The way it always did.

Everything seemed so right this time, so perfect.

'I know,' she said.

His nose touched hers. 'I want to be inside you.'

The heat in his gaze burned away the last of her fears as her fingertips brushed the thick arousal already tenting the fabric of his trousers.

'I know.'

Gripping her fingers, he headed towards the bedroom, hauling her behind him.

And she let her heart soar.

Dane didn't question the frantic need driving him to claim her, possess her. Because he couldn't. Not any more.

The sight of her in the designer dress, its sleek material sliding over slender curves, watching the sultry knowledge in her mermaid's eyes, had been driving him wild all evening. And the last vestiges of the civilised, sensible guy he'd become had been blown to smithereens—the way they had been every day, one crucial piece at a time, ever since she'd marched into his office a week ago.

This hunger wasn't just lust. He knew that—had known it for days, if he was honest with himself. And for that reason he should just let her go. But he couldn't.

Because she was his—any way he could get her. And the desire to mark her as his, keep her near him, had become overwhelming.

He'd insisted on taking her out to dinner, then tortured them both with a slow dance at the Soca Shack to prove that he could hold it together. That this didn't have to mean more than it should. But he'd felt as if he were holding a moonbeam in his arms as she moved against him—so bright, so beautiful, and still so far out of reach—and it had finally tipped him right over the edge of sanity.

He slammed open the first door he came to—the bathroom suite. Swinging her round, he pressed her up against the tiles, filled his hands with those lush breasts. He sucked her through the shimmering silk of her gown, groaning against the damp fabric when he found her braless.

She bucked against him, her response instant and oh-so-gratifying when he tugged the straps off her shoulders, freeing her full breasts.

He kicked off his shoes and pushed down his pants, his gaze fixed on the ripe peaks of her breasts, reddened from his mouth.

She found his erection, but he dragged her hand away.

'Lose the dress,' he said as he tore off his shirt, and the gruff demand in his voice made the light of challenge spark in her eyes.

'I don't take orders,' she said, sounding indignant, but he could see the hot light of her lust. She understood this game as much as he did—even if it didn't feel like a game any more.

'Lose the dress or it gets ripped off.'

'Oh, for...'

She shimmied out of the clinging silk to reveal the lacy panties he adored. Palming her bottom, he lifted her onto the vanity unit, shoving her toiletries off the countertop. The bag crashed to the floor, scattering her stuff across the tiles.

Need careered through his system along with pain and possession—the same damn combination that had tortured him a lifetime ago.

She placed trembling palms on his chest. 'Dane, slow down.'

'In a minute,' he said, the need to have her, to claim her, powering through him like a freight train.

He ripped the delicate panties. And plunged his fingers into the hot, wet heart of her at last.

She sobbed, gasped and grasped his biceps. He stroked the slick flesh, knowing just how and where to touch her to send her spiralling into a stunning orgasm. He watched her go over, and the powerful emotion coiling inside him—part fear, part euphoria—made his erection throb harder against her thigh.

'You ready for me?' he demanded, barely able to speak as need tormented him.

She nodded, dazed. He sank into her to the hilt, the euphoria bursting inside him as she clasped him tight.

Yes. If this was the only way he could have her, the

only way he could make her his, he was going to show her that this was one thing no other man would ever be able to give her.

She clung to his arms as he thrust hard and dug deep, her muscles milking him as she started to crest again. The hunger gripped him, as painful as it was exquisite. He shouted out as she sobbed her release into his neck. And his seed burst into the hot, wet grip of her body.

The wish that they could create another baby and then she'd *have* to be his was savage and insane. Just the way it had been all those years ago.

Reality returned as he came down, tasting the salty sweat on her neck, and the first jabs of shame and panic assaulted him. Hell, he'd taken her like an animal. He should have held back. He didn't want her to know how much he needed her.

He eased out of her. Felt her flinch.

'Did I hurt you?'

She was trembling. 'No, I'm fine.'

The words pulsed in his skull. Mocking him and making him ache at the same time. He forced an easy smile to his lips and turned on the hot jets of the shower. Steam rose as he checked the temperature.

'Let's get cleaned up.'

He dragged her under the spray with him. But as he washed her hair, feeling the strands like wet silk through his fingers, that need consumed him all over again. To hold her, to have her, to make her stay.

And the visceral fear that had lurked inside him for so long roared into life and chilled him to the bone.

* * *

'Is everything okay?'

Xanthe watched Dane leave the shower cubicle and grab a towel, feeling his sudden withdrawal like a physical blow.

He wrapped the towel round his hips. 'Sure,' he said, but he didn't turn towards her as he bent to pick up the toiletries scattered over the floor.

The joy that had been so fresh and new and exciting a moment ago, when he'd taken her with such hunger and purpose, faded. She turned off the shower and pulled one of the fluffy bath sheets off the vanity unit to wrap around herself, suddenly feeling exposed and so needy.

Had she completely misjudged everything? All the signals she'd thought he'd been sending her this evening that there might be more? That his feelings matched her own?

'I'll do it.' She stepped towards him to help pick up her toiletries, but he shrugged off her outstretched hand.

'I made the mess. I'll clean it up.' He placed the bag on the vanity unit, dumping the last of its scattered contents inside.

The strangely impersonal tone sent a shudder through her. She wrapped the towel tighter. Then lifted another towel to dry her hair.

'Where are the birth control pills?'

The clattering beat of her heart jumped into an uneasy rhythm at the flat question. 'Sorry?'

'Your pills? You said you were on the pill,' he prompted. 'I don't see them here.'

He'd checked her toiletries for contraceptive pills?

Agony twisted in the pit of her stomach. Slicing through the last of the joy.

'I'm not on the pill.'

His brows arrowed down in a confused frown. 'So what type of birth control are you using?'

She could see the accusation in his eyes, hear the brittle demand in his voice, and all the blurred edges came together to create a shocking and utterly terrifying truth.

She'd been wrong—so wrong—all over again.

'I'm not using any,' she said.

'What the hell—?'

He looked so shocked she felt the hole in the pit of her stomach ripped open—until it was the same gaping wound that had crippled her once before.

He marched towards her and gripped her arm. 'What kind of game are you playing? Are you *nuts*? I could have gotten you pregnant again.'

She tugged her arm free, the accusation in his face cutting into her insides. How stupid she had been to keep this a secret. When it was the thing that had grounded her for so long. Stopped all those stupid romantic dreams from destroying her.

'I'm not going to get accidentally pregnant. Because I can't.'

She walked past him, suddenly desperate to get away from him. She needed to have some clothes on and to get out of here.

'Wait—what are you saying?' He followed her out of the bathroom and dragged her round to face him.

She thrust her forearms against him. 'Let me go. I want to leave.'

She tried to wrestle free, but he wouldn't let go.

'You need to tell me what you mean.'

She could feel the storm welling inside her, tearing at her insides the way it had for so many years while she'd struggled to come to terms with the truth. But she didn't want to break in front of him. She had to be in control, to be measured, not let him see how much this had devastated her when she told him the details—or he would know she'd fallen for him again. And the one thing she could not bear was his pity.

'I told you—I can't get pregnant.'

'Why can't you?'

The probing question was too much.

'What gives you the right to ask me that?'

'Hell, Red, just tell me why you can't have another child. I want to know.'

The storm churned in her stomach, more violent than the one they'd survived together, and tears were stinging her eyes.

'Because I'm barren. Because I waited too long in that motel room to call my father. I was sure that you would come for me. I was haemorrhaging. There was an infection. Understand?'

She headed towards the lounge, frantic now.

'I need to leave. I should have left yesterday.'

This time she held back the tears with an iron will. Pity, responsibility, sex—those were the only things Dane had ever had to give. She could see that so clearly now.

'Why didn't you tell me?' His voice sounded strained.

'Because it happened and now it's over,' she said.

She got dressed while he watched. Grateful when he didn't approach her. She was stronger now. She could get through this. She wasn't the bright, naive girl she'd once been—someone who'd come close to being destroyed by her past. She could never let him have that power over her again.

Shoving the few meagre items she had brought with her into her briefcase, she turned to look at him.

He stood in the doorway, the towel hooked around his waist, his expression frozen and unreadable.

'You know what's really idiotic?' she said. 'For a moment there I thought we could make this work. That somehow we could overcome all the mistakes from our past, all the things we did wrong, and make it right.'

'What?'

He looked so stunned she hesitated—but only for a moment. This was a ludicrous pipe dream. It always had been and always would be.

'It was a stupid idea,' she said. 'Like before.'

She wanted to be angry with him, so she could fill the great gaping hole in the pit of her stomach. But she couldn't. Because all she could feel was an agonising sense of loss.

'Damn it, Red. I'm sorry. I didn't mean to hurt you.'

He approached her and lifted his hand, but she stiffened and stepped back.

'Can't you see that just makes it even more painful?' she said.

He let his hand drop. His expression wasn't frozen any more. She could see confusion, regret, maybe even sadness, but she steeled herself against the traitorous wobble in her heart that made her want to believe they still had a chance.

She pulled the papers out of the briefcase. The papers she'd come all this way to make him sign in order to end their marriage, without ever realising that what she had really wanted to do was mend it.

'You expected me to trust you, Dane. And you got angry when I didn't. But despite all the confusion with these—' she lifted the papers and dropped them on the coffee table '—the truth is I do trust you. And I think I always did. Because I never stopped loving you. That's why it's so ironic that you were never able to trust me.'

His jaw flexed. His gaze was bleak. But he didn't try to stop her again as she walked out the door.

She felt herself crumpling. The pain was too much. But she held her body ramrod-straight, her spine stiff, until she climbed into a cab to take her to the airport.

She collapsed onto the seat, wrenching sobs shuddering through her body.

'You all right, ma'am?' the cab driver called through the grille.

'Yes, it's okay. I'm okay,' she murmured as she scrubbed away the tears with her fist and tried to make herself believe it.

She *would* be okay. Eventually. The way she had been before. Dane was a part of her past. A painful, poignant part of her past. She'd just forgotten that for a few days.

He'd never been a bad man. He had simply never been able to love her. Not the way she needed to be loved.

Once she was back in the UK—back where she belonged, doing what she loved—everything would be okay again.

But as they headed to the dock, and the boat to Nassau, even the promise of a fifteen-hour workday and her luxury apartment overlooking the Thames couldn't ease the lonely longing in her battered heart—for something that had only ever been real in her foolish romantic imagination.

CHAPTER SEVENTEEN

'BILL SAYS THEY'RE ready to sign off on the Calhoun deal. He's checked through the contracts and everything looks good.'

'Right. Thanks, Angela,' Xanthe murmured as she studied the small pleasure boat making its way up the Thames.

July sunlight sparkled off the muddy water, reminding her of…

'Is everything okay, Miss Carmichael?'

Xanthe swung round, detaching her gaze from the view out of the window of her office in Whitehall to find her PA studying her with a concerned frown on her face. The same concerned frown Xanthe had seen too often in the last two weeks. Ever since she'd returned from the Bahamas.

Get your head back in the game.

'Yes, of course.' She walked back to her desk, struggling to pull herself out of her latest daydream.

Everything *wasn't* okay. She wasn't sleeping, she'd barely eaten a full meal in two weeks, and she felt tired and listless and hollow inside.

Maybe it was just overwork. After the… She paused to think of an adequate word… After the *difficult* trip to the Caribbean, she'd thrown herself back into work as soon as she'd returned. She'd wanted to be busy, to feel useful, to feel as if her life had purpose, direction—all those things she'd lacked so long ago when she'd allowed herself to fall into love with Dane Redmond the first time.

But work wasn't the panacea it had once been.

She missed him—not just his body and all the wonderful things he could do to hers, but his energy, his charisma, the dogged will, even the arrogance that she'd once persuaded herself she hated. Even their arguments held a strange sort of nostalgia that made no sense.

Their trip had only been five days in total. Her life, her outlook on life, couldn't change in five days. This was just another emotional blip that she would get over the way she'd got over all the others.

But why couldn't she stop thinking about him? About the feeling of having his arms around her as she wept for their baby? The force field of raw charisma that had energised everything about their encounter and made everything since her return seem dull and lifeless in comparison?

And that look on his face when she'd told him of her foolish hopes… He'd looked astonished.

Every night since her return she'd lain awake trying to analyse that expression. Had there been disbelief there? Disdain? Or had there been hope?

Angela slipped a pile of paperwork onto the desk blotter. Then pointed at the signature field on the back page. 'You just need to sign here and here, and I'll get it back to Contracts.'

Xanthe picked up the gold pen she used to sign all her deals. Then hesitated, her mind foggy with fatigue and confusion. 'Remind me again—what's the Calhoun deal?'

She heard Angela's intake of breath.

When her PA finally spoke, her voice was heavy with concern. 'It's the deal you've been working on for three months…to invest in a new terminal in Belfast.'

Xanthe wrote her signature, the black ink swimming before her eyes, the tears threatening anew.

Good Lord, why couldn't she stop going over the same ground, reanalysing everything Dane had said and done? Trying to find an excuse to contact him again?

This was pathetic. *She* was pathetic.

The intercom on her desk buzzed. She clicked it on as Angela gathered up the documents and began putting them back into the file. 'Yes, Clare?' she said, addressing the new intern Angela had been training all week.

'There's a gentleman here to see you, Miss Carmichael. He says he has some papers for you. He's very insistent. Can I send him in?'

'Tell him to leave them outside.' She clicked off the intercom. 'Could you handle it, whatever it is, Angela? I think I'm going home.'

'Of course, Miss Carmichael.'

But as Angela opened the door Xanthe's head shot up at the low voice she could hear outside her office, arguing with the intern. Her mind blurred along with her vision at the sight of Dane striding into her office.

'Excuse me, sir, you can't come in here. Miss Car—'

'The hell I can't.'

He walked past Angela, who was trying and failing to guard the doorway.

'We need to talk, Red.'

Xanthe stood up, locking her knees when her legs refused to cooperate. A surge of heat twisted with a leap of joy, making her body feel weightless. She buried it deep. Shock and confusion overwhelmed her when he marched to the desk, his muscular body rippling with tension beneath a light grey designer suit and crisp white shirt.

'What are you doing here?'

Hadn't she made it clear she never wanted to see him again? Couldn't he respect at least *one* of her wishes? She couldn't say goodbye all over again—it wasn't fair.

Pulling a bunch of papers from the inside pocket of his suit, he slapped them down on the desk. 'I've come to tell you I'm not signing these.'

'Shall I call Security?' Angela asked, her face going red.

If only it could be that simple.

'That's okay, Angela.'

'I'm her husband,' Dane growled at the same time.

Angela's face grew redder. 'Excuse me…?'

'I'll handle this,' Xanthe reiterated. Somehow she *would* find the strength to kick him out of her life again. 'Please leave and shut the door.'

The door closed behind her PA as heat she didn't want to feel rushed all over her body and her heart clutched tight in her chest. She glanced down at the crumpled papers. Their divorce papers. The ones she'd tried to make him sign to protect her company.

'If you've quite finished bullying my staff, maybe you'd like to explain to me why you found it necessary to come barging in here to tell me something I already know.'

She'd had new papers drawn up as soon as she'd returned. Papers without the codicil.

'Dissolving our marriage is merely a formality now,' she said, trying to keep the panic out of her voice. She couldn't argue about this now—not when she was still so close to breaking point. 'In case your lawyer hasn't told you, I've filed new papers,' she added. Maybe this was simply a misunderstanding. 'There's nothing in them you should find objectionable. I trust you not to sue for the shares. You've got what you wanted.'

'I know about the new papers. I'm not signing those either.'

'But… Why not?' Was he trying to torture her now? Prolong her agony? What had she done to deserve this punishment?

'Because I don't want to,' he said, but he didn't look belligerent or annoyed any more. His features had softened. 'Because you matter to me.'

'No, I don't—not really,' she said, suddenly feeling desperately weary. And sad.

Did he think she wanted his pity? Maybe he was trying to tell her he cared about her. But it was far too little and way too late.

'Don't tell me how I feel, Red.'

'Then please don't call me Red.'

The sweet nickname sliced through all her defences, reminding her of how little she'd once been willing to settle for. And how she'd nearly persuaded herself to do so again.

He walked round the desk, crowding into her space. She stiffened and tried to step back, but got caught between the chair and the desk when his finger reached out to touch a curl of hair.

'I came here to ask you to forgive me,' he said. 'For being such a monumental jerk about pretty much everything.'

She drew her head back, her heart shattering, the panic rising into her throat. 'I can't do this again. You have to leave.'

Dane looked at Xanthe's face. Her valiant expression was a mask of determination, but the stark evidence of the pain he'd caused was clear in the shadows under her eyes that perfectly applied make-up failed to disguise. And he felt like the worst kind of coward.

He'd spent the last fortnight battling his own fear. Had come all this way finally to confront it. He had to risk everything now. Tell her the truth. The whole truth.

'I don't want to dissolve our marriage. I never did.'

It was the hardest thing he had ever had to say. Harder even than the pleas he'd made as an eight-year-old in that broken-down trailer.

'I love you. I think I always have.'

She stilled, the pants of her breathing punctuating the silence. The sunlight glowed on the red-gold curls of her hair. But then the quick burst of euphoria that

he'd finally had the guts to tell her what he should have
told her a decade ago died.

'I don't believe you,' she murmured. She looked wary
and confused. But not happy. 'If you had ever loved me,'
she said, her voice fragile but firm, 'you would be able
to trust me. And you never have.'

He felt a tiny sliver of hope enter his chest, and he
who had never been an optimist, nor a romantic, never
been one to explain or justify or even to address his
feelings knew he had one slim chance. And no matter
what happened he wasn't going to blow it.

'I do trust you. I just didn't know it.'

'Don't talk in riddles. You didn't trust me over the
miscarriage—you thought I'd had an abortion. And you
didn't trust me not to get pregnant again. For God's
sake, you even searched my toiletries.'

'I know. But that was down to me and stuff that happened long before I met you. I can see that now.'

'*What* stuff that happened?'

Oh, hell.

He might have guessed Xanthe wouldn't take his
word for it.

He stood back, not sure he could explain himself
with any clarity but knowing he would have to if they
were going to stand any chance at all.

'You asked me once a very long time ago what happened to my mother.'

'You said she died when you were a child—like mine.'

He shook his head. How many other lies had he told
to protect himself?

'She didn't die. She left.'

* * *

'What? When?'

Xanthe stared blankly at Dane as he ducked his head and braced his hands against the desk. She felt exhausted, hollowed out, her heart already broken into a thousand tiny fragments. He'd said he loved her. But how could she believe him?

'When I was a kid.' He sighed, the deep breath making his chest expand. 'Eight or maybe nine.'

'I don't understand what that has to do with us.'

He raked his fingers over his hair, finally meeting her eyes. The torment in them shocked her into silence.

'I didn't either. I thought I'd gotten over it. I missed her so much, and then I got angry with her. But most of all I convinced myself I'd forgotten her.'

'But you hadn't?'

He nodded, glanced out of the window.

Part of her didn't expect him to explain. Part of her wasn't even sure she wanted him to. But she felt the tiny fragments of her heart gather together as his Adam's apple bobbed and he began to talk.

'He hit her, too, when he was wasted. I remember she used to get me to hide. One night I hid for what felt like hours. I could hear him shouting, her crying. The sound of...'

He swallowed again, and she could see the trauma cross his face. A trauma he'd never let her see until now.

'She was pregnant. He slapped her a couple of times and went out again. To get drunker, I guess. When I came out she was packing her stuff. Her lip was bleeding. I was terrified. I begged her to take me with her. She said she couldn't, that she had to protect the baby. That I was big enough now to look out for myself until she could come back for me.'

His knuckles turned white where he held the edge of the desk.

'But she never did come back for me.'

Was this why he had always found it so hard to trust her? To trust anyone? Because the one person who should have stayed with him, who had promised to protect him, had abandoned him?

'Dane, I'm so sorry.'

Xanthe felt her heart break all over again for that boy who had been forced to grow up far too fast. But as much as she wanted to comfort him, to help him, she knew she couldn't go back and make things better now.

'Don't be sorry. It was a long time ago. And in some ways it made me stronger. Once I'd survived that, I knew I could survive anything.'

'I understand now why it was so hard for you to ever show weakness.'

And she *did* understand. He'd had to survive for so long and from such a young age with no one. His self-sufficiency was the only thing that had saved him. Why would he ever want to give that up?

'But I can't be with someone who doesn't need me the way I need them. It was like that with my dad. And it was the same way with us. I waited too long to call him that day because I didn't want to betray you.'

Her voice caught in her throat, but she pushed the

words out. She had to stand up for herself. For who she had become. She couldn't be that naive, impressionable girl again. Not for anyone.

'I love you, Dane. I probably always will. You excite me and challenge me and make me feel more alive than I've ever felt with any other person. But I can't be with you, make a life with you, if we can't be equal. And we never will be if you always have to hold a part of yourself back.'

But as she opened her mouth to tell him to leave he took her wrists, first one, then the other, and drew her against him. He touched his forehead to hers, his lips close to hers, his voice barely a whisper. Tension vibrated through his body as he spoke.

'Please give me another chance. I loved that girl because she was sweet and sexy and funny, but also so fragile. I thought I could protect her the way I could never protect my mom. And I love knowing that some of that cute, bright, clever kid is still there.'

He pressed his hand to her cheek, cradled her face, and the tenderness in his eyes pushed another tear over her lid.

'But don't you see, Dane? I can't be that girl any more. You walked all over me and I let you.'

He wiped the lone tear away with his thumb. 'Shh, let me finish, Red.'

The lopsided smile and the old nickname touched that tender place in her heart that still ached for him and always would.

'What I was going to say was, as much as I loved that girl, I love the woman she's become so much more.'

She pulled back, scared to let herself sink into him again. 'Don't say that if it isn't true.'

'You think I told you about my mom to make you feel sorry for me?'

She shook her head, because she knew he would never do that—he had far too much bullheaded pride. 'No, of course not. But…'

He touched his thumb to her lips. 'I told you because I want you to know why it's taken me so damn long to figure out the obvious. The truth is I was scared witless, Red. Of needing you too much. The way I'd once needed her. But do you know what was the first thing I felt when you walked into my office and told me we were still married?'

'Horror?'

He laughed, but there wasn't much humour in it. 'Yeah, maybe a little bit. But what I felt the most…' His lips tipped up in a wary smile. 'Was longing.'

'That was just the sex talking.'

His hands sank down to her neck. 'Yeah, I wanted to believe that. We both did. But we both know that's a crock.'

She ducked her head, but he lifted her chin.

'I love that you're your own woman now. That you're still tender and sweet and sexy, but also tough and smart enough to stand up to me, to never let me get away with anything. We're likely to drive each other nuts some of the time. I'm not always going to be able to come clean about stuff. Because I'm a guy, and that's the way I work. But I don't want to sign those papers. I want to give our marriage another chance. A *real* chance this time.'

'But I live in London and you live in New York. And we—'

'Can work anything out if we set our minds to it,' he finished for her. 'If we're willing to try.'

It was a huge ask with a simple answer. Because she'd never stopped loving him either.

'Except…I can't have children naturally. But I want very much to be a mother.'

'Then we'll check out our options. There's IVF, adoption—tons of stuff we can look at.'

'You'd be willing to do all that for me?' His instant commitment stunned her a little.

'Not just for you—for me, too. I want to see you be a mother. I always did. I was just too dumb to say so because I was terrified I wouldn't make the grade as a father.'

She sent him a watery smile, stupidly happy with this new evidence of exactly how equal they were. While she'd been busy nursing her own foolish insecurities she'd managed to miss completely the fact that he had some spectacularly stupid ones, too.

'Hmm, about that…maybe we should look at the evidence?' she teased.

'Do we have to?' he replied, looking adorably uncomfortable.

'Well, you're certainly bossy enough to make a good father.' Her smile spread when he winced. 'And protective enough, and tough enough, and playful enough, too.'

She pressed herself against him, reached up to circle

her arms round his neck, tug the hair at his nape until his mouth bent to hers.

'I guess we'll just have to work on the rest.'

'Is that a yes?' He grinned, because he had to be able to see the answer shining in her eyes through her tears. Her happy—no, her *ecstatic* tears. 'You're willing to give this another go?'

'I am if you are.'

His arms banded round her back to lift her off the floor. 'Does that mean we get to have lots of make-up sex?' he asked.

His hot gaze was setting off all the usual fires, but this time they were so much more intense. Because this time she knew they would never need to be doused.

'We're in my office, in the middle of the day. That would be really inappropriate.'

His grin became more than a little wicked as he boosted her into his arms. 'Screw *appropriate*.'

EPILOGUE

'YOU GRAB THAT ONE… I've got this one.'

Xanthe laughed, scooping up her three-year-old son, Lucas, before he could head for the pool while she watched her husband dive after their one-year-old daughter who, typically, had crawled off in the opposite direction.

Rosie wiggled and chortled as her favourite person in all the world hefted her under his arm like a sack of potatoes—very precious potatoes—into the beach house that stood on a ridge overlooking the ocean.

After facing their third round of IVF, almost two years ago now, she and Dane had embarked on the slow, arduous route to adoption. The discovery a few months later that Xanthe was pregnant, in the same week they'd been given the news that they'd been matched with a little boy in desperate need of a new home, had been like having all their Christmases come at once, while being totally terrifying at the same time.

They would be new parents with *two* children. But could they give Lucas the attention he needed after a tough start in life while also handling a newborn?

Xanthe could still remember the long discussions they'd had late into the night about what to do. But once they'd met Lucas the decision had been taken out of their hands. Because they'd both fallen in love with the impish little boy instantly. As quickly as they'd later fallen in love with his sister, on the day she was born.

'Mommy, I want to do more swimming,' Lucas demanded.

'It's dinnertime, honey,' Xanthe soothed as her son squirmed. 'No more swimming today.'

'Yes, Mommy—*yes*, more swimming!' he cried out, his compact body full of enough energy to power a jumping bean convention—which was usually a sign he was about to hit the wall, hard.

'Hey, I'll trade you.' Pressing a kiss to Rosie's nose, Dane passed her to Xanthe. 'You give the diaper diva her supper and I'll take the toddler terminator for his bath.'

Dane nimbly hoisted their son above his head.

'Come on, Buster, let's go mess up the bathroom.'

'Daddy, can we race the boats?'

'You bet. But this time I get to win.'

'No, Daddy, I *always* win.'

Lucas chuckled—the deep belly chuckle that Xanthe adored—as Dane bounced him on his hip up the stairs of the palatial holiday home they'd bought in the Vineyard, and were considering turning into their permanent base.

Dane had already moved his design team to Cape Cod, and was thinking of relocating the marketing and sponsorship team from the New York office, too. His busi-

ness was so successful now that clients were prepared
to come to him.

Xanthe allowed her gaze to drift down Dane's naked
back, where the old scars were barely visible thanks to
his summer tan, until it snagged on the bunch and flex
of his buttocks beneath the damp broad shorts as he
mounted the stairs with their son. The inevitable tug
of love and longing settled low in her abdomen as her
men disappeared from view.

Extracurricular activities would have to wait until
their children were safely tucked up in bed.

Rosie yawned, nestling her head against Xanthe's
shoulder, and sucked her thumb, her big blue eyes blink-
ing owlishly. She cupped her daughter's cheek. The
flushed baby-soft skin smelled of sun cream and salt
and that delicious baby scent that never failed to make
Xanthe's heart expand.

'Okay, Miss Diaper Diva, let's see if we can get some
food into you before you fall asleep.'

After a day on the beach, trying to keep up with her
daddy and her big brother while they built a sand yacht,
her daughter had already hit that wall.

Ella, their housekeeper, arrived from the kitchen, as
the aroma of the chicken pot pie she'd prepared for the
children's evening meal made Xanthe's stomach growl.

'Would you like me to feed her while you take a
shower?'

'No, we're good.' Xanthe smiled.

In their late fifties, and with their own children now
grown, Ella and her husband John had been an absolute godsend when she'd gone back to work—taking

care of all the household chores and doing occasional childcare duties while she and Dane concentrated on bringing up two boisterous children and running two multinational companies with commitments in most corners of the globe.

'Why don't you take the rest of the evening off? I've got it from here,' Xanthe added. 'That pie smells delicious, by the way.'

'Then I'll get going—if you're sure?' Ella beamed as Xanthe nodded. 'I made a spare pie for you and Dane, if you want it tonight. If not just shove it in the freezer.'

'Wonderful, Ella. And thanks again,' she said.

The housekeeper gave Rosie a quick cuddle and then bade them both goodbye before heading to the house she and her husband shared in the grounds.

As Xanthe settled her daughter in the highchair she watched the July sunlight glitter off the infinity pool and heard wild whooping from upstairs. Apparently Dane and their son were flooding the children's bathroom again during their boat race.

The sunlight beamed through the house's floor-to-ceiling windows, making Rosie's blonde hair into a halo around her head. Xanthe's heart expanded a little more as she fed her daughter. To think she'd once believed that her life was just the way she wanted it to be. She'd had her work, her company, and she'd persuaded herself that love didn't matter. That it was too dangerous to risk her heart a second time.

Her life was a lot more chaotic now, and not nearly as settled thanks to her many and varied commitments. They had a house on the river in London, and Dane's

penthouse in New York, as well as this estate in the
Vineyard, but as both she and Dane had demanding
jobs and enjoyed travel they rarely spent more than six
months a year in any of them.

As a result, their children had already climbed the
Sugarloaf Mountain, been on a yacht trip to the Sey-
chelles and slept through the New Year's Eve fireworks
over Sydney Harbour Bridge. Eventually she and Dane
would have to pick one base and stick to it, which was
exactly why Dane was restructuring his business and
why she'd appointed an acting CEO at Carmichael's in
London, giving herself more flexibility while oversee-
ing the business as a whole.

But with Dane's nomadic spirit, her own wander-
lust, and their children still young enough to thrive on
the adventure, they'd found a way to make their jet-set
lifestyle work for now.

By risking her heart a second time she had created
a home and a family and a life she adored, and discovered in the process that love was the *only* thing that really mattered.

Rosie spat out a mouthful of food, looking mutinous
as she stuffed her thumb into her mouth.

Xanthe grinned. 'Right, madam, time to hand you
over to your daddy.' She hauled her daughter out of the
highchair and perched her on her hip. 'He can read you
a bedtime story while I feed your brother, and then rescue the bathroom.'

And once all that was done, when both her babies
were in bed, she had *other* plans for her husband for
later in the evening.

She smiled. Love mattered, and family mattered, but sometimes lust was pretty important, too.

'How do you feel about taking the munchkins to Montserrat next month?'

'Hmm…?' Xanthe eased back against her husband's chest as his words whispered into her hair and his hands settled on her belly.

The sun had started to drift towards the horizon, sending shards of light shimmering across the ocean and giving the surface of the pool a ruddy glow. She felt gloriously languid, standing on the deck. The children were finally out for the count, and Ella's second chicken pot pie had been devoured and savoured over a quiet glass of chardonnay.

The adult promise of the evening beckoned as warm calloused fingertips edged beneath the waistband of her shorts.

'Montserrat? Next month?' he murmured, nipping at her earlobe. 'I've got to test a new design. Figured we could rent a house…bring Ella and John along to help out with the kids while we're working. We might even get some solo sailing time.'

She shifted and turned in his arms, until her hands were resting on his shoulders and she could see the dusk reflected in his crystal blue eyes.

'Sounds good to me,' she said. 'As long as we have a decent internet connection I can handle what I need to on the Shanghai development.'

She pressed her palms to the rough stubble on his cheeks and sent him a sultry grin which made his expression darken with hunger.

'But right now all I want to handle is *you*.'

His lips quirked, his challenging smile both promise and provocation. 'You think you can *handle* me, huh?'

Large hands sank beneath her shorts to cup her bare bottom and drag her against the solid ridge forming in his chinos.

Arousal shot to her core, staggering and instantaneous. 'Absolutely,' she dared.

'We'll just see about that,' he dared back, as he boosted her into his arms.

She laughed as he carried her into the house, then took the steps two at a time to get to their bedroom suite. But after he'd laid her on the bed, stripped off her clothes and his, his gaze locked on hers and her heart jolted—she could see all the love she felt for him reflected in his eyes.

'You're a witch.' He trailed his thumb down her sternum to circle one pouting nipple. 'A sea witch.'

She groaned as he cupped her naked breasts.

'But you're *my* damn sea witch.'

She bucked off the bed as he teased the tender peak with his teeth.

'Perhaps you should use your superpower to make sure I never forget it,' she said breathlessly.

'Damn straight,' he growled, before demonstrating to her, in no uncertain terms, just how thoroughly she belonged to him, while she gave herself up to the passionate onslaught and handled everything he had to offer just fine.

* * * * *

*If you enjoyed this story, why not try
Heidi Rice's previous books?
They're sassy, stylish and supersexy!*

**ONE NIGHT, SO PREGNANT!
UNFINISHED BUSINESS WITH THE DUKE
PUBLIC AFFAIR, SECRETLY EXPECTING
HOT-SHOT TYCOON, INDECENT PROPOSAL
PLEASURE, PREGNANCY AND A PROPOSITION**

Available now!

#3509 PURSUED BY THE DESERT PRINCE
The Sauveterre Siblings
by Dani Collins

When Prince Kasim finds he's falsely accused Angelique Sauveterre of an affair with his future brother-in-law, he can't resist this feisty beauty himself! Angelique blossoms under Kasim's touch and surrenders. But can he give her more than passion and precious jewels?

#3510 THE TEMPORARY MRS. MARCHETTI
by Melanie Milburne

Cristiano Marchetti proposes to Alice Piper to fulfil the conditions of a will. But his real agenda is revenge—for leaving him years ago! That is until it seems the future Mrs. Marchetti might become more than Cristiano's *temporary* bride...

#3511 THE SICILIAN'S DEFIANT VIRGIN
by Susan Stephens

Luca Tebaldi is furious at Jennifer Sanderson for inheriting his brother's estate—he'll seduce the truth out of her! But this sensual innocent sets Luca's senses on fire, forcing him to confront what *she* is enticing out of *him*!

#3512 THE FORGOTTEN GALLO BRIDE
by Natalie Anderson

Zara Falconer's wedding to Tomas Gallo set her free, but an accident wiped Tomas's memory before he could annul their vows. When she discovers this tortured man is still her husband, she has to ask—will their passion bring back Tomas's memories?

Raul Di Savo desires more than Lydia Hayward's body—his seduction will stop his rival buying her! Raul's expert touch awakens Lydia to irresistible pleasure, but his game of revenge forces Lydia to leave... until an unexpected consequence binds them forever!

Read on for a sneak preview of
Carol Marinelli*'s 100th book,*
THE INNOCENT'S SECRET BABY,
the first part of her unmissable trilogy
BILLIONAIRES & ONE-NIGHT HEIRS.

Somehow Lydia was back against the wall with Raul's hands on either side of her head.

She put her hands up to his chest and felt him solid beneath her palms and she just felt him there a moment and then looked up to his eyes.

His mouth moved in close and as it did she stared right into his eyes.

She could feel heat hover between their mouths in a slow tease before they first met.

Then they met.

And all that had been missing was suddenly there.

Yet the gentle pressure his mouth exerted, though blissful, caused a flood of sensations until the gentleness of his kiss was no longer enough.

A slight inhale, a hitch in her breath and her lips parted, just a little, and he slipped his tongue in.

The moan she made went straight to his groin.

At first taste she was his and he knew it for her hands moved to the back of his head and he kissed her as hard as her fingers demanded.

More so even.

His tongue was wicked and her fingers tightened in his thick hair and she could feel the wall cold and hard against her shoulders.

It was the middle of Rome just after six and even down a side street there was no real hiding from the crowds.

Lydia didn't care.

He slid one arm around her waist to move her body away from the wall and closer into his, so that her head could fall backward.

If there was a bed, she would be on it.

If there was a room, they would close the door.

Yet there wasn't and so he halted them, but only their lips.

Their bodies were heated and close and he looked her right in the eye. His mouth was wet from hers and his hair a little messed from her fingers.

"What do you want to do?" Raul asked while knowing it was a no-brainer, and he went for her neck.

She had never thought that a kiss beneath her ear could make it so impossible to breathe let alone think.

"What do you want to do?" He whispered to her skin and blew on her neck, damp from his kisses, and then he raised his head and met her eye. "Tonight I can give you anything you want."

Don't miss
THE INNOCENT'S SECRET BABY,
available March 2017 wherever
Harlequin Presents® books and ebooks are sold.

HARLEQUIN
Presents®

We can't wait for you to read *Secrets of a Billionaire's Mistress* by Sharon Kendrick—a tale of inescapable passion! Darcy and Renzo are about to experience a romance like no other…

Waitress…

Neither tall, willowy nor sophisticated, waitress Darcy Denton knows she isn't Renzo Sabatini's usual type. But, enthralled by the powerful magnate, unworldly Darcy becomes addicted to their passionate nights together.

Mistress…

Ensconced in Renzo's secluded Tuscan villa, Darcy glimpses Renzo's troubled past and desolate soul. She knows she should end it before she gets in too deep—but then she discovers she's pregnant!

Wife?

Harboring her own childhood secrets, Darcy dare not tell Renzo. But as the mother of his child it's only a matter of time—nine months, to be exact—before he claims what's his…

Don't miss

SECRETS OF A BILLIONAIRE'S MISTRESS

Available March 2017

Stay Connected:

www.Harlequin.com

f /HarlequinBooks

🐦 @HarlequinBooks

P /HarlequinBooks

HP06045

REQUEST YOUR FREE BOOKS!

HP15